The Ice Elf & The Fire Elemental

An Ice Elf Fantasy

Book 2

Leah R Cutter

Reviews

It's true. Reviews help me sell more books. If you've enjoyed this story, please consider leaving a review of it on your favorite site.

Come someplace new...

Do you enjoy exploring strange new worlds, new cultures, new people? Sign up for my newsletter and I'll start you on your travels with a free copy of my book, *The Island Sampler*.

http://www.LeahCutter.com/newsletter/

Buy More!

Did you know that you can buy directly from the Knotted Road Press website?

https://www.knottedroadpress.com/shop/

Also by Leah R Cutter

Cozy Fantasy

A Dragon's Guide to Killing Gods (And Other Lies)

Custom Dwarven Chocolates

The Ice Elf & The Snow Cone

The Ice Elf & The Fire Elemental

Cozy Paranormal Mystery

The Water Witch Mysteries

The Witch is Inn

To Scratch a Witch

Witches and Waterways

Grilled Sand and Witches

Witch Mirror?

Urban/Contemporary Fantasy Series

Seattle Trolls

The Changeling Troll

The Princess Troll

The Fairy-Bridge Troll

The Troll-Demon War

The Troll-Human War

The Troll-Troll War

The Witch's Progress

Circle of Air
Circle of Fire
Circle of Water
Circle of Earth

The Shadow Wars Trilogy

The Raven and the Dancing Tiger
The Guardian Hound
War Among the Crocodiles

The Clockwork Fairy Kingdom

The Clockwork Fairy Kingdom
The Maker, the Teacher, and the Monster
The Dwarven Wars

The Cassie Stories

Poisoned Pearls
Tainted Waters
Spoiled Harvest
Bloodied Ice

The Chronicles of Franklin

Franklin Versus The Popcorn Thief
Franklin Versus The Soul Thief
Franklin Versus The Child Thief

Epic Fantasy Series
The Fallen Elves

Chapter One

Elbriarien sighed with relief when she glanced over the edge of the cliff, down the path. The scenic view partway down the rock face, overlooking the harbor, appeared to be unoccupied. Though it was the middle of the work week, and not a rest day, she'd still worried that a family might have snuck off to have a picnic on this beautiful, late spring morning.

Clouds dotted the blue sky with the precision of a master artist. The water beyond the yellowed, limestone cliffs sparkled in the sunlight. Ships with multiple masts and sails moved leisurely, like grand old aunties too dignified to run anymore. Even the wind cooperated, only gusting now and again instead of a steady onshore blow.

She looked over at Mara who carried their picnic basket. While El, as an Ice Elf, was much stronger than a Human, Mara, as a fire elemental, was even stronger, and so had insisted on bearing the weight. She didn't look that strong, though, being much shorter than El, her body athletically slim and ethereally beautiful. She had a thin face with a pointed nose, sharp chin, and classically high cheekbones. Her golden skin glowed in the light of the sun. Amber eyes held joy now, instead of sorrow. She wore her auburn hair up in a messy bun, with two silver sticks poking out, each having little silver charms of snow cones dangling from them. El had given them to her as a Longest Night present—and had received in return a necklace with a fire opal that she wore constantly.

Today, Mara dressed in a short red-orange tunic with no sleeves and brown trousers that went down to her calves. Sturdy sandals wound their way around her feet and up muscular calves.

Mara gave El a big smile that warmed her heart, then El turned and started down the path to the overlook.

Everything *had* to go well today. El had a speech planned and red promise-ribbons tucked away in one of the pockets of her white cotton dress. Though she was no longer in the cold north, she still wore long sleeves and robe-like dresses that went down to her ankles, with an equally long vest, today's being sage-colored, like the little shrubs dotting the ground. She kept herself cool using a cantrip, basically, a bit of magic native to Ice Elves that would automatically keep her warm enough in the north, or cool enough down here, on the southern-most tip of the continent.

As they wound down the steep incline, El started hearing noises. The wind constantly shifted directions, so she wasn't exactly certain what they were and where they were coming from. Was there some sort of wild animal up ahead?

Nothing dangerous would wander this close to the large city of Osirholm. Plus, between her ice magic and Mara's fire magic, they could take care of themselves.

Only as they grew close to the overlook that El realized people *were* already occupying the spot and that the noises were coming from them.

Bedroom noises.

Elves, and in particular, Ice Elves, did not blush. El certainly didn't. She had more control than that.

Her cheeks may, *perhaps*, have grown a bit warm when she realized what the couple who'd gotten there ahead of them was doing in such an isolated, secluded location.

El turned to Mara and indicated that they needed to go back up the trail.

Mara didn't move, but gave her a teasing grin instead.

"Ye sure about that, lass? Could join 'em, have some fun," Mara said.

El's cheeks did *not* grow warmer at the suggestion.

"No, thank you," she said stiffly.

Mara giggled but obligingly turned around and started heading back up the hill.

Which gave El the change to watch Mara's delicious form all the way to the top and try hard *not* to think about what the couple below were doing.

"Ye want to just have our picnic 'ere?" Mara asked, indicating the top of the trail. "That way we can see who was below. Give 'em a round of applause as they walk by."

El shook her head. "No, I don't want to know who is down there. What if it's one of our friends?" Though El had only been in Osirholm for a year, she'd still met a lot (*a lot*) of people, thanks to her Human friend Kucher, who appeared to be on a first-name basis with at least half the city. He ran *The Book Ends* inn with his wife Nel, who was an Umber Elf from the Tiriandi Desert north and east of the city.

"If we know who it is, we can be happy for 'em," Mara said seriously.

"I'd rather just assume that they're finding their joy, than to know for certain," El said dryly.

Mara shrugged. "Up to ye."

El wasn't sure if Mara really didn't know if waiting (and applauding!) wasn't appropriate, or if she was still teasing.

Mara had been carved out of fire by the Dwarf Thatur Icemaster. He'd been trying to expand his magical abilities and not be just an Ice Mage, but also a Fire Mage. He'd only partially succeeded. His initial act of creation had left both him and Mara crippled. He'd died soon afterward, and it wasn't until Mara had absorbed the power from a fire demon that she was able to become a full fire elemental herself.

In many ways, that meant that Mara had only recently been born. She'd stepped out of the flames and become a person just two and a half years ago. Sometimes, people and their customs were beyond her understanding. Other times, she seemed surprisingly wise, as if she held the wisdom of the hearth.

"Let's see if there's another picnic spot over there," El said. She'd actually planned for this, in case her first choice of location was occupied.

It took the pair of them three tries before they found an empty, quiet, yet scenic spot for their picnic.

El was adamantly *not* frantic by that time. No, she'd faced down ice demons. Squabbling siblings. Mothers frantic to get their children treats at the snow cone business that she and Mara ran together.

She could surely survive a delay in her plans.

Mara helped El spread out the blanket and set the containers of food on it. They had cold chicken from their meal the night before, seasoned with lemon, thyme, and pepper. El had picked up garlic bread sticks from the market that morning. Fresh strawberries and blueberries filled one of the little bowls. And of course, they carried a little bit of shaved ice with one of the new syrups that Vorwin, the Gnome cook had invented: a blackberry syrup that had been cooked with spices that made El's tongue go zing.

"Now, we gonna eat or ye gonna talk first?" Mara said casually after everything was settled.

El rolled her eyes at herself. Of course, Mara had sensed that something was up. Despite how others might view El as glacially cold, with the beauty and elegance of an Elf, her lover knew better.

El should have known not to try to keep a secret from Mara.

She paused, looking over the spread before them, out at the beautiful water, then turning to look at the beautiful fire elemental beside her. Then she shook her head. Mara might be right—the words she had to say might choke her throat, making it impossible to eat anything.

Though her hands were steady, her heart beat in her ears as strongly as if she faced an ice demon alone, with no spells prepared. She knelt up on the blanket, then motioned for Mara to do the same, so they faced each other.

She drew Mara's always warm hands into her own, holding them together before her chest.

"I know we haven't known each other that long. Particularly given how long we both may live." Elves regularly lived five hundred years or more. No one knew how long a fire elemental had. Possibly Mara was immortal, her flame eternal.

"But I love you, and I want to spend the rest of my days with you," El said all in a rush.

"I love ye, too," Mara said, sounding wary. "What exactly are ye asking?"

"Will you marry me?" El said. "Or at least be promised to me, and be my betrothed?"

Mara looked away.

El's heart sank.

"You don't have to if you don't want to. I know I'm rushing into this a bit," El said, letting go of Mara's hands and drawing back, sitting on her heels. "I just thought that you might feel the same about me."

"Ack, come here, ye silly goose," Mara said, grabbing El's hands and holding them fiercely in her own, drawing her back up to her knees.

"I love ye. I've been thinkin' about this, too. I do want to spend the rest of my days with ye," Mara said.

"But?" El said. "I know there's a *but* in there somewhere." She told herself not to feel crushed. Mara hadn't said *no*.

At least not yet.

"But," Mara said, pausing and taking a deep breath before she continued, "what all's involved in gettin' married? Or even betrothed?"

"Well, I have promise bracelets that I made for us out of red ribbons," El admitted. "We wear those to start, to indicate that we've chosen one another. Then, when we decided the time is right, we gather our families together and meet with one of the priestesses of the moon. She performs a ceremony and marries us."

"Aye, there's the rub," Mara said. "Who's me family?"

"Uhm," El said, a stumbling a bit. "It doesn't have to be your actual, biological family. It could be a chosen family. Like Sigder and Wyne, or Kusher and Nel."

"And the ceremony, it's all icy, right?" Mara said.

"Oh," El said. She obviously hadn't thought the whole thing through. She'd been so focused on actually proposing that she hadn't considered the ceremony.

"It doesn't have to be," El said. "We could change it, to more reflect fire."

Mara gave her a brittle smile. "So we have a priest of fire with a priestess of the moon? How would that work, exactly? Ye know as well as I do that our magic isn't compatible. And yer supposed to have some spells performed then, right?"

El nodded. It was one of the sticking points between them. Their magic was literally fire and ice. Though El would love to be able to do magic with Mara, they hadn't found a way to make it work.

Yet.

"So, lass, how about we do this?" Mara looked away, out over the cliff. She took a deep breath before she turned back to El, her face a pensive scowl. "I don't mind being promised to ye. And the bracelets ye brought are red, right?"

El freed one of her hands and drew them out of her pocket. She'd taken shiny red ribbons, made from silk, then braided them together using complicated knotwork. (She didn't want them to accidentally fall apart. That would be bad luck.) One end of each bracelet had a ribbon ball, the other, a loop, so the bracelets could be put on and taken off easily.

Traditionally, they weren't supposed to be taken off. However, both El and Mara worked at *Ice & Berries*, their snow cone shop. She didn't want the ribbons to get all gunky.

"I should have made yours red and orange," El said when she didn't see instant delight in Mara's eyes. The fire elemental regularly wore both red and orange, now that she'd come fully into herself. El still preferred whites and off-whites, with pastel blues and greens. (Vorwin frequently muttered under her breath about El being *beige* but they were still good friends.)

"That would have been better, yes," Mara admitted. "But ye did go to all this work. I need to acknowledge that."

El took the offending bracelets and shoved them back into her pocket. "I'll remake them," she said.

Mara nodded solemnly. "With orange. And blue. The promise bracelets shouldn't just reflect fire, but ice as well."

El swallowed down her hurt. Plain red was traditional. It was something she'd dreamed about for her betrothal.

However, this was for her and Mara. It didn't have to be traditional. Everything needed to be as special and unique as they were.

"However, before I put on yer promise bracelet, I need to talk with Thatur's folks," Mara said seriously. "A Dwarf must get permission from their elders afore getting engaged. Or promised. Or whatever."

El's eyes widened. While Mara wasn't a Dwarf, she had, in many ways, been raised as one, as was evident in her accent.

"Of course," she said. "I apologize for rushing into things this way."

"Ach, yer young," Mara said.

That got the eyeroll it deserved. While El was technically in her seventies, she'd also grown up in the frozen north and hadn't experienced much of the world beyond fighting the ice demons before she'd arrived in Osirholm.

"We'll take it slow. Do it our way. Then yes, at the end, I'll marry ye," Mara said.

El's heart caught and started beating hard again when Mara kissed her.

She was going to have to figure out how to take Mara's feelings into account every step of the way. The pair of them would have to create their own special ceremony.

She was up for the challenge.

Chapter Two

El had been reticent to tell anyone about proposing to Mara. Though she'd been certain the fire elemental would say yes (and she technically, kind of had) El had wanted it to be a surprise, something she could flaunt when the pair of them met with their friends.

So it shocked El when she walked into *The Book Ends* inn the following day and the first thing Nel asked was, "So? How did it go? Let me see your promise bracelet!"

It was late afternoon, and the tavern at the front of the inn had just opened for business. No one crowded around the tables scattered across the open floor. Nel stood behind the bar that ran the entire length of the room on the left. Two huge kegs were suspended from the ceiling on thick iron chains above the flat expanse. Clay pots and glass bottles, all holding different types of liquor for creating drinks, lined the shelves on the wall.

El reluctantly held up her arm, showing that she only still had her Mage Mark around her wrist (two silver bands, which indicated that she could legally do magic).

"Oh, I'm so sorry," Nel said.

"How did you know?" El asked. "I didn't tell you anything!"

Nel just chuckled as she stepped further into the light. "Did you really think you were hiding anything?"

While both El and Nel were Elves, being thin, tall, graceful, and with pointed ears, their similarities ended there.

El's skin was as white as freshly fallen snow, and her hair was long and chestnut-brown. Nel's skin so black she blended into shadows even without magic. She had red eyes that burned like two coals in the dimness of the tavern. Though Nel wasn't that old, her hair was as white as an elder's, spiked all around her head as though she'd gone down to the shore and let the wind style it. She wore a tight, sleeveless tunic the soft gray of mourning doves. Gold rings pierced the entire outer edge of her right ear, and a glittering blue gem at least two inches across hung around her neck.

El paused for a moment, horror washing over her. "Wait. Does Kucher know?"

While the tavern on the main floor of *The Book Ends* inn could be considered a local hotspot in terms of gossip, Kucher was a walking, talking, rumormonger. Though he was Human, he had friends among all the different races whom he talked with daily.

If he knew, then at least half of Osirholm also knew.

"Naw, I wouldn't do that to you," Nel said with a sly smile. "Particularly not until after you had your bracelets on. What happened?"

El sighed, letting herself relax a bit. "Mara said yes, but not right yet."

"Go on," Nel said, encouraging El to take a seat at the bar

while Nel busied herself behind it, making a quick pot of tea for the pair of them.

"Mara's a fire elemental," El said. "As an Elf, I have all sorts of ceremonies and traditions to choose from when it comes to our betrothal. She...doesn't. And we want to make a ceremony that's meaningful for both of us."

"I see," Nel said. She wrapped her hands around the teapot, instantly bringing it to a boil. Mara could do the same thing. It was something that El had always been slightly envious of: instant hot water for tea.

Whereas she could always cool a hot drink down, making ice out of just about any liquid. (Some alcohol became more like a slush than frozen solid, which had surprised her. Something to do with how strong it was.)

"What did you and Kucher do?" El asked. It had been one of the main reasons why she'd stopped by the inn that afternoon, at a time when she knew that it wouldn't be too crowded and she could just chat with Nel for a while.

As Nel was an Umber Elf, and Kucher was a Human, they must have made some changes to their wedding ceremony, right?

Nel gave her a fond smile, her eyes growing distant as she remembered. "Kucher got me a promise ring at first," Nel said. "That's the Human tradition."

El glanced down at Nel's hands. No obvious ring adorned her fingers. "Uhm—do you still have it?"

Nel reached up and brushed her right ear. "Had it made into these," she said with a grin as she pointed out the dozen or so small gold rings that pierced the flesh there.

"Huh," was all El had to say to that. She wasn't even sure what to ask next.

"It's a custom among the Umber Elves to pierce their ears,"

Nel said. "And that ring was so big, had so much gold in it, Kucher had it reforged into many smaller ones. Not all of these came from the original ring, but most of them."

"Interesting," El said. "And your wedding ceremony?"

"Ceremonies," Nel corrected as she poured both of them a cup of tea.

El obligingly took a taste as Nel directed.

It tasted smoky, which was the Umber Elf's preference. In the desert where she'd grown up, the tea was cured over a wood fire. Under that, a sweet-sour taste coated El's tongue. If she was guessing right, it came from dried apricots that had been added to the blend. Then came the astringency of the black tea itself, slightly puckering her tongue. All that was followed by smoothness and a warmth at the back of her throat. Just a thimbleful of brandy had been added, barely enough to taste, more to just get the presence of it, like a ghost warming her tongue before it disappeared.

"Lovely as always," El said.

When Nel had learned of El's upbringing, and the distinct lack of spice she'd experienced, the Umber Elf decided to take it upon herself to educate El's tastebuds, making different teas and flat breads for El to try.

They sat for a while in the darkened room, sipping their tea, before El spoke up. "You said ceremonies?"

"Yup," Nel said. "We had two. One done by the head moon priestess, out in the desert, Umber Elf style. Then a second one, here in Osirholm, done Human style."

She reached up and touched the necklace she always wore. The blue gem in the center of it was smooth on the surface but still roughly cut, not symmetrical. Silver encased the edges of it, and it hung from a silver chain that was as thick as El's pinky.

"This wasn't part of the Human ceremony, but something

promised at it," Nel explained. "Lapis lazuli, which is precious to my people. As part of the Human ceremony, we promised each other gifts in a year's time. Kucher had this made. I gave him a special apricot ale, made by a master Umber Elf brewer. I get him a small bottle every year, for our anniversary."

"Mara doesn't have any family. Or traditions, as a fire elemental," El pointed out. "We are going to visit the Icemasters, the elders of Thatur's family, to ask for permission to marry."

"Does Mara want to get married in a Dwarven style?" Nel asked.

"No, I don't think so. Though I don't know the Dwarven traditions. Do you?" El asked.

Nel shrugged. "Seems to involve a lot of drinking, going from one tavern to the next. We've had a few wedding parties come through here."

"I'll be sure to ask," El said.

When El had first come to Osirholm, she'd started off working as a tutor for Gyles and Ceceline Margravine. They hadn't parted on the best of terms, though El did regularly stay in touch with Brytha, their Dwarven housekeeper, as well as the cook, Vorwin. Finmore, Sigder and Wyne's tutor, came by the shop with them often. Sigder and Wyne still made money from the shop monthly, coming up with new ideas of things to try to keep the business not just surviving but thriving.

"You'll figure out something special," Nel said. "You just have to listen to each other, make sure that it's not just traditional, but *your* traditions."

"We will," El promised.

Nel grew thoughtful for a moment. "Have you thought about—" Nel started to say when Kucher came barging in.

"Hey, beautiful, look what I brought you!" he said triumphantly. "Oh, hi, El!"

"Hi, Kucher," El said.

The Human looked like many others in the city, at least to El's eyes: short, squat, and muscular. He wore his fiery orange hair shaved close to his skull, though his mustache of the same color was looking particularly bushy that day. As usual, he only wore brown overalls with no shirt underneath, his arms bulging with strength.

While Kucher was showing off the strawberry brandy he'd found in the market, the first of the regulars started rolling into the tavern. El forgot that Nel had a question for her, and instead, slipped out of the tavern as its owners took care of their customers.

El had already gotten the ribbons to remake the promise bracelets, though she'd held off on reknotting them. She wanted to make sure that she got it right, instead of rushing into things as she first had. Plus, they still had to visit the Dwarves before Mara would wear hers, a visit that they'd put off for the time being.

El was determined to be patient, though.

Her marriage to Mara was worth waiting for.

Chapter Three

The weather slid from spring to summer, which was the busiest time for the *Ice & Berries* shop. Everyone wanted cool treats during the warm days. Plus, Vorwin appeared to have out-done herself with the latest syrups that they poured on the shaved ice. They kept a basic rotation of eight different flavors, and each one had customers who proclaimed it was the best they'd ever tasted.

They'd put their promising and the wedding on hold. El assumed that they'd wait until fall before making their visit to the Dwarves, though she didn't ask Mara about it directly.

Both El and Mara were busy in the shop that afternoon—one of the usual rushes that occurred most workdays, after children were finished with their lessons and before the evening meal. During the usual dinner time for people in Osirholm there would be a lull in the shop. Then they'd get slammed with business again, as people came to the shop for an after-meal treat.

El remembered when she'd first come to the shop: Mara

didn't have a menu or a system for making the syrups. Like El, Mara hadn't ever developed her tastebuds much.

Since becoming a full fire elemental, Mara had been able to taste many more flavors than she had. In addition, her eyesight had improved. When she'd only been a sliver of a fire elemental, she couldn't distinguish between as many colors as El could.

This made Mara's initial choices for syrups unfortunate, as she didn't have any idea of what would look amazing as well as taste divine.

Now, Mara was turning into an artist when it came to creating and decorating their iced treats. She wasn't as good as El—she wasn't an Elf with the innate sense of design that all Elves had. Mara was still making much better choices than she used to when it came to decorating her creations, adding sprinkles, drizzles of fruit, or even crushed cookies, a new treat that had only recently made its way onto their menu.

Nilafels—the Dwarven war machine originally created to produce ice and snow to fight ice demons—continued to work much better, now that El was in charge of it. While Mara could now run the machine using magic, as well as keep it clean, it still seemed to prefer El, and wouldn't get clogged as frequently when she ran it.

The machine had never been in battle. Its exterior was a pristine, bright red, with delicate blue filigree lines decorating it. El didn't know if the machines she'd worked with up north had been painted such colors and the paint had all chipped off, or if the Dwarves hadn't bothered decorating them. The front of Nilafels had been greatly modified from the war version of the machine. Instead of a single large opening that would shoot out a winter storm, there were three silver spigots, each about the size of her palm. Knobs, buttons, and dials adorned the space above and below them, letting the user of the machine control the speed the ice was produced, as well as the desired consistency.

El worked with Nilafels that afternoon, behind the counter with Mara, filling bowls with the specified ice (crushed, flaked, or shaved). Bokkel—a local Dwarf they'd hired—worked the front of the shop, cleaning up customer tables (though most people did bus their own dishes) as well as directing new customers to the beautiful menus painted on the wall and updated quarterly by Sigder. Though Bokkel was shy, and didn't speak much, particularly for a Dwarf, she still smiled readily at the customers and made them feel welcome.

As far as El could tell, Bokkel wasn't directly related to Thatur Icemaster, but they were cousins of some sort. (She hadn't wanted to delve into the matter, as Dwarven family genealogies were a complicated tangle of lineages. She was certain it would take Bokkel more than an hour to explain the exact relationship, not that the Dwarf would make the effort to speak so much. So "cousins" was a close enough approximation.)

As the rush subsided and customers trickled down to just a few, a female Dwarf walked in. She held herself back from the line, gazing at Mara working hard behind the counter. The Dwarf wore a beautiful, heavily tooled leather vest, an off-white shirt with puffy sleeves, and short pants. Her black-and-gray curly beard was trimmed in gold and silver nuggets, and rings covered all her fingers. The heavy wrinkles across her brow and around her eyes indicated she was old for a Dwarf.

El doubted that the mysterious Dwarf was royalty, however, she probably was someone from an important family.

Mara stiffened when she finally looked up.

El was at her side in an instant. "Who is that?" she asked quietly.

"Snalgrud Icemaster. Thatur's eldest sister," Mara replied, her voice barely above a whisper.

"Did you know she was coming?" El had to ask.

Mara pressed her lips together. "I requested permission to call on the Dwarven elders. To talk with them about yer proposal," she said.

El blinked, surprised. She hadn't realized that Mara had taken some steps toward their future. She'd thought the whole thing had just been put off until fall, when the shop wouldn't be as busy.

"So, I was expectin' an answer. Not a visit," Mara finished off with.

Snalgrud appeared to have satisfied herself that Mara knew she was there, and so joined the end of the line. Only two people were in front of her, so she didn't have to wait long.

"Yer busy," Snalgrud said as way of greeting.

"Aye, sister," Mara replied. "But not so much, now. Can take a break whiles most are eatin' their dinner."

Snalgrud just sniffed at her.

El was *not* going to snap at the Dwarf. This Snalgrud should be proud of Mara, happy that she'd continued in the business that Thatur had set up for her.

"So what's this concoction?" Snalgrud asked after gazing down at the bottles filled with syrup sitting behind the counter.

Mara explained the concept of the shop, how people could order different varieties of ice, syrup, and sprinkles.

"Ye make a good profit, don't ye?" Snalgrud said, nodding. "Particularly on these warm days."

"Aye," Mara said, with just a touch of smugness.

"But what about when the winter winds blow?" Snalgrud continued.

"We don't serve as many iced treats, then," Mara admitted. "We sell hot drinks at that time, along with baked goods." She indicated the case beside her that held just a few cookies at this point.

"Bake 'em here?" Snalgrud asked.

"Some," Mara said. "Some we get at a discount from one of the bakers in the night market."

The Dwarf just continued to look at everything, not speaking.

A few more people joined the line behind her.

"Is there something ye'd like to try?" Mara said eventually.

"Dragon's breath. On flaked ice," Snalgrud said. "With some of those gold toppings."

El hid her smile as Mara rushed to fulfill the Dwarf's order.

A lot of the Dwarves who came through ordered that exact combination. Something about the colors that appealed to them, the red and the gold.

"I'll take over," El told Mara as she finished the treat.

"Thanks, love," Mara said as she took the dessert out from behind the counter and indicated that Snalgrud should follow her to the very back of the shop, where they could continue to chat with some vague privacy.

As an Elf, El could have strained her ears to hear what they were saying.

She wouldn't stoop to spying on her partner, though.

They chatted through the dinnertime lull. Bokkel washed the dishes in the kitchen behind the counter while El handled all the customers, cleaning up and bringing a few more dishes back.

The shop was just starting to get busy when Mara and Snalgrud stood up and walked through the shop. They stopped at the counter for a moment.

"Snalgrud Icemaster, I'd like you to meet Elbriarien Itamar, my partner," Mara said formally.

El stood up straight, then bowed formally to Snalgrud. "It is a pleasure to make your acquaintance."

"She's a fancy one, tain't she?" Snalgrud said to Mara in a gruff voice.

"Aye. But I'm a keeping her," Mara said with one of her brilliant smiles, the kind that made El grateful that she was an Ice Elf and didn't blush. Despite how warm her cheeks grew.

"You come see us, up in Zaharbun, when the rains start," Snalgrud said. "The family will get you time with the Dwarven elders, let you make yer case to them." She gave first Mara, then El a sharp nod and practically marched out of the shop.

"Everything okay?" El asked Mara as she slipped behind the counter to join her.

"I think so," Mara said. "The Dwarves, well, they don't have the warmest feelings for the Elves. But I'm not really a Dwarf, either. So I think we'll be all right."

She sounded worried as she looked out the door.

"We'll be fine," El said.

She knew that it was important to Mara to get the approval of the Dwarven elders for their marriage.

So she'd do whatever she needed to make it happen.

Chapter Four

Between working at the shop, preparing for their trip, and just generally living their lives, El didn't have a lot of time to do spell research. While she knew that her former master, the Dragon Azutjengaban, would demand that she needed to find the time for such important work, she also didn't feel compelled to obey his strictures anymore.

No, she needed to do the spell research for herself and for Mara.

Their magic didn't work or play well together, as they were literally fire and ice.

Fortunately, now that El had her Mage Mark, she had unfettered access to the largest spell library in the city, maintained by the Woodland Elves.

She waited that evening, lying in bed with Mara as her lover slept. The moon was full and El felt its gentle light calling to her outside the warm room.

The place hadn't changed much since she'd moved in. Maybe a few more decorations hung from the wooden walls and a few more clothes hung in the beautifully carved wardrobe that stood next to the bed. The hearth that took up one of the back corners now felt like the heart of their small space. They hadn't bothered with a bigger bed, as they found that they enjoyed sleeping practically on top of one another.

At the same time, Mara had never removed the small rocking chair that had once been Thatur's, which stood in the far corner. The shelves that took up one of the walls still contained some of his wood-working tools. While Mara would always mourn the death of her creator, the grief felt a lot less heavy, now. It was pushed to the side and lived on the edges of their lives, not front and center.

One of the things that had surprised El was that Mara still needed to sleep like a Human, even with her full power.

Like most Elves, El could go without sleep for two or three nights before she started to feel the effects. On the other hand, Mara needed sleep every night, or her internal fires would dim.

El had no idea if that was a leftover from when Mara hadn't had her full power, or if all fire elementals were like that.

She'd found a book in the library that had contained a lot of knowledge about the four types of elementals: fire, water, earth, and air. But it had been more of an overall guide about how to survive an encounter with an elemental and not about their personal habits.

Though elementals weren't monsters and wouldn't automatically attack someone who came into their territory, they didn't suffer fools at all, according to the book. Anyone pestering them was not likely to survive.

El would have thought that the fact that fire elementals slept through the night would have been an important enough tidbit to be recorded, but perhaps it wasn't general knowledge.

There had been a chapter in the book about the potential for ice elementals, but that had eventually been disproven: the being in question had been someone's creation, not an elemental itself.

Just as there were four types of elementals, there were four types of demons, though they were different: ice, fire, acid, and smoke. (The type labeled as a fire demon was actually a lava demon, though they rarely were allowed to live long enough to achieve their final form and spew molten rock.)

The origins of all the known elementals were cloudy, as some seemed to give birth to themselves while in their element, whereas others were given form by magic, like Mara was.

Much more scholarly work had been done about demons. Demons came from another plane of existence and were always waiting for an excuse to leave and wreak havoc on alternative planes.

It had been well determined that a spell that went awry was the vehicle that demons most often used to travel between the planes. In part, that was why the King's Law existed, why it had been illegal for El to do complicated spells and magic without her Mage Mark.

However, now she had her mark. And Mara, as a fire elemental, fell outside of the law. She was a magical being, like an Elf. The vast majority of her magic flowed naturally from her. She didn't need to cast a spell, use expensive ingredients, or come up with a specific chant in order to do magic. She just willed things into being. She could also just see magic, something that El had had to be trained to do.

While El had cantrips she could use for very small magic, she needed spells to do any big magic.

El and Mara had tried playing with simple bits of magic together, but everything El created would be quickly canceled by Mara, or vice-versa. (So. Much. Water. Everywhere!)

Hence, El's weekly visits to the Elven library, to seek out a spell they might be able to do together.

When El was certain that Mara was deeply asleep, she slipped from their bed then went out the window. The air outside was cooler than the day had been and smelled of wood smoke from nearby hearths. Clear skies held stars that were outshone by the full moon. El paused for a moment breathing in the peace of the night, before she went up the small rope ladder that went from their bedroom window to the roof. From there, El could silently leap between buildings, delighting in her passage, before finally landing on the single-story house down the block, then lightly jumping down to the street.

This neighborhood of Osirholm had a regular night watch, as well as magical lights that decreased the shadows. Not eliminated them—not just the Elves but others would object to that. Only the Humans needed the lights in order to see. Some, like the Dwarves and the Umber Elves, actually didn't do as well in bright daylight.

El quickly passed through the streets, skipping up two flights of stairs to get to higher levels of Osirholm, then through a tangle of streets before reaching the Elven enclave.

There were four types of Elves on the continent of Annund: Ice, Umber, Woodland, and Alpine. They could roughly be aligned with the elements of water, fire, earth, and air.

As Woodland Elves primarily inhabited the Elven enclave, a mass of trees blocked the front of it.

El wasn't challenged as she made her way up the path winding between the massive trunks. Golden lights twinkled high in the canopy—not really enough to see by, but comforting, even homey, at least to an Elf. The cool air smelled of baked pine needles and dried mulch. When the rainy season came, El would join the mushroom hunts that the Elves conducted amongst the giant trunks.

While the other races were welcome to pass time in the woods and the beautiful gardens tucked away on either side of the path, few were allowed past the stone gates, made out of majestically carved rocks brought there by the Alpine Elves.

The gates loomed far above El's head as she approached. Magical blue lights danced along the geometric shapes that made up the pillars. She saw a guard's head peek over the crenulated top, then disappear again.

No one challenged El's right to go into the enclave, particularly at night. As far as El knew, she was the only Ice Elf in the entire city. That just made her an oddity, not unwelcome. More than one of the elder scholars living in the enclave had stopped by her table in the library while she'd been doing spell research. They would politely ask a few questions about her and her kind, as they'd never met an Ice Elf before, before moving along and allowing her to get back to her studies.

The main building of the enclave was built out of living trees, grown together with magic. It stood three stories tall, with a roof open to the sky. (At least during the dry season. Beautiful magical fabrics acted as a roof during the months it rained.) Mostly evergreens had been used, their sharp needles and massive boughs forming impenetrable walls. It always made El shiver when she saw them, a fierce protectiveness woven into their branches. While of course, any place could be attacked or even burned down, it would take a lot to destroy the enclave.

Grand doors that rose far above El's head stood wide open as she walked up, golden light spilling out onto the path. Soft music came from the ballroom to the right of the entrance hall, some sort of party. Maples, birches, elms, oaks, willows, and other trees that had leaves that changed color in the fall decorated the inside of the wide-open space. Stairs made from still-living branches lined the walls on either side of the entrance, leading up to the second and third levels. Tinkling fountains brought joy to her heart, the air soft and moist. The starlight and moonlight seemed accentuated tonight, mingling with the magical lights, bringing more of a glow to the open area.

El followed the route she knew best, going to her left, then up to the second floor and back a ways to the library of spell books. There was more than one library on this floor, but she was doing spell research that night, not looking for more information about elementals or reading up on the history of Osirholm.

She thought she was close to adapting a spell that she and Mara could cast together. It was an encasing spell that surrounded something in impervious ice. She was going to have to heavily modify it, as the spell was originally a destructive spell that shrank over time, eventually destroying whatever was contained within it.

Perhaps, though, she could cast an ice holder, and Mara could throw a bit of flame into the center of it, and they'd have a physical manifestation of the pair of them, done magically.

The library had a spicy smell, reminding her of the expensive ingredients used for an extravagant spell. It was a square room, not much bigger than the *Ice & Berries* shop, able to hold thirty people comfortably. Stone shelves lined most of the walls, with a few tables in the center. The old books were all magically preserved, as timeless as the solid flagstones that made up the floor. Soft nooks and small reading spaces had been carved out along the sides, hidden between the shelves.

El quickly found the spell book she was looking for and made herself comfortable at one of the tables, writing down the spell she'd been thinking about, along with some of the modifications that she'd come up with, mainly shrinking it down from a cage that could contain an ice demon to something that would fit in her palm.

The spell felt lopsided once she was finished. She wasn't certain what was wrong with it, but her gut told her that it wasn't complete.

"Maybe thicken the walls a bit more?" came a quiet voice just over her left shoulder.

El didn't start. She was an Ice Elf and had better control than that. She did look over her shoulder to find Danasaer—one of the scholars she'd talked with before—standing there.

Woodland Elves had skin the colors of trees, from pale white to golden brown. Danasaer looked more like driftwood, a soft gray color that looked aged and weathered. Black eyes peered out from beneath bushy white eyebrows (that looked as though they belonged on a Human or a Dwarf, quite frankly, though El would never say anything so rude to him). A few lines marred the planes of his face, showing his extreme age, as did the white hair that flowed like a curtain down his back.

"How thick?" El asked, also quiet. Though she didn't think anyone else was there in the library with them, the place still demanded discreet tones.

"Start with a finger-width, and go up from there," Danasaer suggested.

El nodded and drew another sheet of paper toward her. The magical pens that the library accumulated were a wonder, and never ran out of ink.

El redrew the spell, keeping the ratios she needed for ingredients but adjusting them, along with changing a few lines of the chant.

"Better," Danasaer said. "Uhm, I was wondering..."

"Yes?" El prompted him when he didn't continue.

"What is this for, exactly?" Danasaer asked, his confusion showing as he drew his bushy eyebrows together. "It isn't either an offensive or defensive spell."

"You're correct," El said slowly. "It's for my partner, Mara. It's so we could maybe do a spell together." Spells, particularly powerful ones like this, shouldn't be cast frivolously. She'd had that pounded into her head since she'd been a child.

Magic wasn't just for fun. Mostly.

"Ah, that explains the protective space in the center," Danasaer said, nodding. He gave her an encouraging smile. "Magic with a partner is important. There have been quite a few who have modified some spell or another to work with a completely non-magical partner."

El gave a sigh of relief. She'd been so afraid that he was going to scold her or something for such an activity.

"So, let's try this…"

Before dawn, with the help of the scholar, El had a working spell.

In exchange for Danasaer sharing his knowledge so freely, she'd agreed that she and Mara would come and have dinner with him the next week. Though he'd ask them a lot of questions, as in many ways, Mara was as unique in Osirholm as El, she knew that the scholar would also be polite about it.

With a light heart, El skipped most of the way back to the shop, ready to start a new day, eager for the next night when they got to try the spell.

Chapter Five

El and Mara sat upstairs in their shared bedroom. The day had been busy and long and they both were a little tired. However, busy days meant more profit, a bit more breathing room for when the rains came and they wouldn't have as many customers.

Using yellow chalk, El had drawn out a protective ring meant to contain the spell. She sat on one side of the circle while Mara sat across from her. The ring seemed like overkill: the spell as she'd modified it didn't have anywhere near as much power as it once did.

Better to be safe than sorry, though.

Elven characters filled the outside edge of the circle. Like all Elven magic, it was both beautiful as well as functional. She'd also sprinkled dried rowan woodchips around the circle, a natural protector ingredient.

"Are ye sure ye can clean it up after this?" Mara said, looking at the circle that lay between them dubiously.

"I am," El assured her. Again. "It's just chalk."

"Not burning anything into the wood floor?" Mara persisted.

"I wasn't planning on that, no," El said dryly. *She* wasn't the one with the fire magic, and it hadn't been *her* who'd accidentally burned the floor the first time they'd tried this.

"All right," Mara said, still sounding slightly huffy. "So what do ye have planned?"

"I want to try to combine our magic," El said. "Do something together."

Mara just shook her head. "Yer ice. I'm fire. We don't mix that way."

"I'd still like to try," El said, continuing with the argument they'd been having for months now.

"Fine," Mara said. "But ye'll have to fix the floor if it goes awry."

"I will," El said.

She wasn't sure why Mara seemed so set against this tonight. She'd at least been grudgingly accepting the previous times they'd tried and failed. Maybe it was because they were both tired.

El explained the spell to Mara, how she'd create a small ice container that Mara could then add a flame to.

It wasn't much. It would only last as long as they held the spell. However, it would be a start, maybe just the first of many spells El could create so that they could use their magic together.

El went first, casting a beautiful bowl of ice in the center of the containment circle. Danasaer had been correct in his estimates of how thick the bowl had needed to be in order for her to have a balanced spell. That was in part due to the structure of the spell, and that she'd not only cut it down in size but in power as well.

The base was a bit bigger than her palm. From there, it grew up about the length of her fingers. Thick walls formed the exterior, with only a small hollow in the center for Mara's fire.

When El finished, she nodded at Mara.

Her turn.

Mara held up her palm and a small flame rose from it, about the size of a candle wick.

That was when they ran into the first problem, namely, Mara getting her fire through the protective circle. It was meant to keep fire (and ice, and water) contained. It didn't like someone trying to cross it with one of those elements.

El finally had to physically smudge the Elven characters of the part of the circle closest to Mara so that she could throw the flame over the edge, into the waiting container.

For a brief moment, the spells appeared to be working. Mara's flame burned steadily in El's ice, the colors refracting through the room.

El shared a smile with Mara. She *knew* they could do it. that they could do magic together, albeit a very small, well-controlled spell.

Then everything went wrong, all at once.

Mara's flame shot up at the same time that the ice container doubled its size.

El quickly cut all the magic she had going to the spell. However, the container and the spell were designed to keep running, at least for a short while, after the magic to it had been cut. (That was an essential part of the original spell, in case the Elf who'd trapped the ice demon had been killed, so the monster wouldn't be able to escape immediately.)

It wasn't enough.

The magic of the ice container appeared to recognize that it was containing something alien to its nature, something it hated, so the container continued to grow, until it was bigger than El's head.

Mara's flame responded, also enlarging, trying to melt the hated ice.

El may have been blaming too much of what was happening on the spells themselves, giving them too much of a consciousness.

However, magic could be finicky. It wasn't all neatly controlled, or controllable.

Mistakes happened.

Mara's flame suddenly shot up, tall enough to touch the ceiling.

El immediately called up ice, dumping the equivalent of a bucketful of snow on the flame.

That would have dowsed a normal fire. On this one, it was like throwing oil on the flame, as it tripled in size.

"Stop!" Mara said. "I've got it."

El threw a quick glance at Mara. She appeared to be struggling slightly, her eyes squinted in concentration, sweat beading her brow.

El didn't throw any more ice or water, but she kept her hands up, ready if necessary.

Mara slowly coaxed the fire down instead of shutting it off abruptly. She didn't speak any words, just held her hand out, palm up, asking the flame to jump back to her.

Eventually, the fire died down and the flame did leap from where it had been sitting to Mara's palm.

The ice container was long destroyed. El's ice and snow now formed a huge puddle in the center of the circle. At least it had stayed put, the circle actually doing its job, despite the smudge mark on the side.

"Ack," Mara said, dismissing the flame and shooting a glance at El. "What was that?"

"I don't know," El said. She sighed, then stood up. "I'll go get a cleaning bucket and rags to soak all this water up."

She hurried down the steep stairs to the kitchen closet where they kept the cleaning supplies, then hurried back up.

Mara still sat where she had been, looking at the ruins of what should have been a bonding time for them both.

"I'm sorry," she said after a minute as El started soaking up the water with a cloth, then wringing it out into the waiting bucket.

El snorted. "Nothing for you to be sorry about. It was my spell that went awry." She still wasn't sure what had happened. For some reason, the container she'd created had overreacted to Mara's flames. She hadn't planned for that happening at all.

"I think I gave ye too hot of a fire," Mara said after a moment.

El just shook her head. "No, I think I didn't dumb down the spell enough."

The ice container had held too much magic. It shouldn't have reacted that way.

"At least ye didn't ruin the floor?" Mara said. "Soak our entire bedroom?"

"Small wonders," El said shooting her a smile. Then she grew serious. "I know our magics are different. But I didn't think they were that incompatible. This shouldn't have happened."

Mara sniffed. "Does it matter that much to ye?"

El sat back on her heels and turned to face Mara. "On a day-to-day basis? No, it doesn't," El said honestly. "But over a lifetime? Particularly as long of a lifetime as we will have together? I think it will. I think that itch to do magic with you will sour."

"Aye," Mara said, nodding. "I understand."

El finished cleaning up the mess they'd made, wiping the last of the chalk circle from the floor, before heading back downstairs to empty the bucket and drop off the cleaning supplies.

She stood for a moment in the kitchen, stymied.

She wanted a cup of tea. But that would mean finding the tinderbox, gathering up some kindling, and starting the stove. (There was a reason the Ice Elves primarily ate cold, raw, and pickled food. And had magical teapots that would warm with just a touch of magic.)

Before she could start her hunt, Mara came in. "Figured ye'd like tea as much as I would," she said. "I'll get the pot."

El nodded and got the tin containing Mara's favorite tea from the many cannisters, along with two mugs. She measured out a good amount of the leaves into the teapot, as she had the feeling they both needed something strong.

Vorwin had left a couple of bottles of wine under the sink, using it in one of the syrups she created. She'd told El that she could help herself, as long as she didn't go too crazy. (El suspected that Vorwin wasn't too worried about it, since El, at least according to Vorwin, was at best *beige*.)

Mara filled the teapot with water, then wrapped her hands around it, instantly boiling the water.

"I wish I could do that," El said, then she actually put her hands over her mouth, ashamed that she'd spoken her envy out loud.

"I know," Mara said, nodding. "We should at least get you a kettle that you can use."

"That's too expensive," she said. "And I rarely drink tea without you."

"True," Mara said as she poured the water into the waiting teapot. "But do ye need the independence?"

"I don't know," El said. "It isn't something I want to decide tonight."

"All right," Mara said.

The tea steeped while they stood there in silence. It wasn't as comfortable as their quiet time together usually was, but El wasn't sure what to say.

Once the tea was ready, Mara poured it into their waiting cups. El immediately picked up her mug, the welcome heat seeping into her hands.

It wasn't that she was cold. Not exactly. Her cantrips kept her temperature constant.

Maybe it was just the comfort of it all.

"I'm sorry," Mara said again after a moment.

"What in the goddess's many names for?" El said, bewildered.

"I gave ye too hot a flame," Mara said.

El shook her head. How could a fire be too hot? "No, it was my fault."

"Ye wanted to do magic with a part of me," Mara said, stubbornly continuing. "I have different fires, ye know."

El stopped and stared at Mara for a moment. "No, I did not know. What are you talking about?"

"See, there's a regular flame, like what I'd use for this beastie, here," Mara said, patting the stove fondly. "There's a different fire, that I might use for a forge," she continued on. "Stronger, hotter, and will burn longer."

"All right," El said. "And the flame you gave me?"

Mara shrugged. "Not an eternal flame, but close enough. A part of me. Right?"

El blinked, considering the implications.

It had been important for her to do magic with Mara, and she'd emphasized that more than once.

So Mara had given her a special flame, not an ordinary one. Something that meant something to her.

El shook her head. No wonder the ice container had reacted that way! She'd designed it to accept a regular flame.

Not a living part of a fire elemental.

"Oh," El said. "I think I get it? Maybe?"

"Would it have worked with a lesser flame?" Mara asked.

El shrugged. "I don't know. But then it wouldn't have meant as much to you, right?"

Mara nodded. "Aye."

El paused, considering the implications. How could she create something that would contain a living flame? Did she even want to? Or did she need to come up with a different idea, a different way for them to meld their magic together?

"Let's go to bed," Mara said.

El, still carrying her tea, followed her lover back up the stairs to their bedroom, mulling over and rejecting possible spells.

"Ye don't need to solve it tonight, lass," Mara said after El sat silent, still cogitating.

"Oh! Sorry," El said.

"We'll be fine," Mara said firmly, taking El's teacup from her, then proving once again just how compatible they could be, leaving the Elf breathless with wonder and full of love.

Though there was still the teeniest, tiniest worry, El tried to smother it as she lay with Mara and eventually, slept.

Chapter Six

The rainy season finally rolled around. El hadn't thought that she'd miss the rain as much as she did. She had to agree with Mara that sometimes the constantly sunny, nice days bothered her, and that she needed cloudy days as well.

Come the end of the work week, they'd be leaving for the Bunagrund Mountain Range and the Dwarven city of Zaharbun, dug deep into the stone there. They may or may not also take a quick jaunt up the mountain, to visit some of the Alpine Elves who lived there, friends of Danasaer who he assured her would welcome them.

That afternoon, they were having a quiet dinner in the shop with Sigder, Wyne, and their tutor Finmore. El didn't know if the children's parents knew where they actually were, or if Finmore was covering for them. She didn't particularly care, to be honest.

They'd closed the shop after the afternoon rush, and wouldn't open up again until later that evening. Bokkel would be working full time while they were gone, along with Sarry, one of Vorwin's numerous relatives. Since it would be the rainy season, the shop wouldn't be as busy, though they'd still have a good crowd seeking warm drinks and sweet baked treats. Frysa, their baking friend, continued to delight them with delicious pastries.

Over the past year, since El had left the employ of the Margravines, Sigder had gone through a growth spurt. The top of the twelve-year-old's head now reached her collarbone. There was a chance he'd be as tall as her one of these days.

Wyne had grown at a slower pace, being only ten at this point. However, both their parents were pretty tall, so El wouldn't be surprised if Wyne had a growth streak of her own shortly.

As the children were still part owners of *Ice & Berries*, a portion of their time together that night involved going over the books, talking about what parts of the business continued to flourish and what, if anything, they should add to the menu.

Vorwin continued to create new syrups for them once a quarter. Wyne explained how angry it had made Mother when someone had tried to hire Vorwin out from under her. Seemed that working in the shop had gained the cook a following.

"Mother's having to pay Vorwin more, not that she wasn't paying her a lot before," Wyne said with a cheeky grin. "Vorwin has been giggling about their negotiation for more than a week."

That just made El snort, remembering her own negotiations with Vorwin for her initial services.

The shop still hadn't gotten around to some sort of loyalty program, rewarding repeat customers, as those customers came back regularly anyway.

Mara did admit to possibly making bigger servings for some of those who were her regulars.

All of the profits that went to the siblings as part of their share for coming up with the initial concepts, for Sigder's painted menus on the walls, and for Wyne's continued inspired advertising campaigns, went into a separate bank account for the youths.

"Mother said we can't touch the money until after we reach our majority," Sigder complained.

El just nodded in sympathy, though privately, she thought it was a good idea. It wasn't significant amounts of money, but it was steadily growing. It would certainly help them set up in their own businesses. She knew that Ceceline Margravine wanted Sigder to take over her business when he got older. He may or may not have been suited to managing a group of scribes. If he could have made his living doing painting and drawing, he probably would have done that instead. However, artists tended to be poor, and his parents were dead set against that happening to him.

Wyne would probably make a better heir for her mother's business, as she had a very good head for numbers and appeared to like contract law.

Maybe Sigder would be better working for his father, instead, as he managed the wine imports for a number of merchants in the city, as well as many of the inns and taverns. However, that would also involve a lot of talking to people, which quite frankly, wasn't Sigder's forté.

Those decisions were many years in the future, though.

For now, all of them had a lovely evening chatting. El and Sigder managed some of the evening's conversation in High Elvish, the language that was common for all of the different types of Elves. He was much better at languages than his sister. However, she was better at numbers, and so was able to dominate part of the conversation discussing percentages and profit forecasts.

Mara had explained the reason for their journey to the children at the start of dinner. Toward the end of dinner, Wyne finally asked, "What type of wedding ceremony will you have?"

El smiled at her. "We don't know yet. We're still figuring that out." Then she paused before she added, "What are the different types of wedding ceremonies?"

She figured that Wyne and Sigder knew about Human wedding traditions, something that she wanted to learn.

She's also assumed that as children, they didn't know everything. However, it would be a start.

"So first, you have to court," Sigder said solemnly. "That means taking your partner out to the market and maybe buying her things, or going on a picnic, or taking her to view the harbor."

"Like you're doing with Illyn?" Wyne asked slyly.

"What? No! Not at all. Nothing like that," Sigder said, growing red in the face. "We're just friends."

"Uh huh," Wyne said, clearly not believing her brother.

"Anyway," Finmore said, smoothing over the two siblings before they fell to more squabbling, "after courting, the proposing party buys a promise ring for the other party."

"Yeah, you should see the one that Father bought Mother," Wyne said. "It's solid gold, and covers her entire finger! She doesn't wear it, of course, but she does bring it out on their anniversary. Puts it on the table like it's a guest or something."

El nodded. She'd wondered how Nel had managed to get so many earrings out of a single promise ring. Evidently, it wasn't meant to be worn.

"In poorer families, the ring isn't that large. But the ring is always deliberately designed to be divided up, so that if the family comes upon hard times, the promise ring will support them, provide some capital when needed," Finmore said. "That way, it isn't just a promise for them getting married, but a promise that they'll be able to provide for one another, throughout the marriage."

"'Poor is the married woman who's run through her promise ring, and still has babes to feed,'" Wyne quoted.

El nodded. It wasn't how the Elves managed their wealth, but for a shorter-lived race like the Humans, it made sense.

"After the promise ring has been accepted, the couple chooses the most auspicious day for their wedding," Sigder said, finally recovered from his embarrassment and determined to take part in the conversation.

"Auspicious?" Mara asked, clearly puzzled. "What does that mean?"

"That's why there are many different types of ceremonies," Wyne said solemnly. "It depends on the couple, what's most important to them."

"Mother and Father got married at the start of the new year," Sigder said. "That way, they could celebrate the start of their new businesses, and grow their wealth more."

"Other people get married closer to the spring solstice," Wyne said. "They want lots of babies."

Sigder sniggered. "'A solstice bride can do in six months what other brides take nine months to do.'"

Mara giggled out loud at that.

While the Elves had no problem with children being born out of wedlock, El was aware that some Humans did.

"Farmers marry their spouses in the fall, to bring them a good harvest," Wyne added.

"And the summer equinox? Do people marry at that time as well?" El had to ask.

"They're like the Dwarves, then. Father likes summer

weddings. People drink a lot more at those sorts of weddings," Sigder assured them.

"They have a certain respect for celebrating," Finmore said, trying to temper the conversation. "For enjoying life, and the living of it."

The children, but mostly Finmore, went into a lot more details about the different ceremonies, different priests and priestesses, different rites.

Mainly, though, it made El wonder when would be the best time of year for her and Mara to get married. Either summer equinox, as a celebration of their life together, or closer to the Longest Night, which was celebrated by the Elves and was the start of their new year.

Mara agreed that those were the most likely times for them, if they were going to be picky about a date.

El went to bed with so many plans, so many thoughts about the future.

The only thing she knew for certain was that she and Mara were still going to take their time and figure out when would be the perfect date for them.

Chapter Seven

Osirholm jutted out of the bottom of the continent of Annund. It was not merely the southernmost city, but also the southernmost tip of land.

The Bunagrund Mountain Range was to the north and slightly west of them. They could either take a ship up the coast, then walk inland to the mountain range, or they could go directly north by foot, along one of the trade routes, then follow the roads to the city.

El would have loved to go by ship, possibly even see if *The Piebald Pup*, the ship she'd taken from the Ice Elves' territory down to Osirholm, was around and could carry them.

However, she couldn't convince Mara to go that route. Mara was afraid she'd drown if there were any sort of accident. She couldn't swim, and there was no amount of coaxing that El could do to get her lover to go into the water. She never went to the baths in town, but instead only ever did a quick wash in the sink to clean herself.

El could understand that, though. Mara was a fire elemental. Fire and water were never going to mix easily.

While they (probably) could have afforded to rent a cart, they decided to walk instead. Neither of them had spent a lot of time in this part of the country. It would be an adventure for them.

A tiring one, as El discovered, after the first two days of walking along wet, muddy roads. Though it was just the start of the wet season, the rain had been heavy in the area, and the land wasn't used to so much water. Not many people traveled the same roads they did. (They didn't learn until they were already well on their way that most merchants waited out the first couple of weeks after the rains began before they started their journeys. The rains were always heaviest at the start of the season.)

Fortunately, inns were spread out along the way, and so they didn't have to camp out at night, at least not yet. They were prepared to do so if they decided to. Between the pair of them, they had enough magic to keep themselves warm and dry.

Mara had traveled this way with Thatur after he'd imperfectly drawn her from the flames. She didn't really remember the road, though. They'd hired a cart, and she'd spent much of the time in the covered back with the injured Dwarf, seeing to his needs.

El took heart in the slow change of scenery. At first, everything was fairly flat, with small brush, scrub oaks, and prickly weeds along the edges of the road. Hills appeared first, undulating slightly, though still covered with the same (lack) of greenery.

The first clear day dawned as forests gathered on the very edge of the horizon. The weather had grown cooler, too, as they'd traveled north.

They decided to spend that night sleeping along the edge of

the road, possibly even in the trees, if they could make it that far.

"Do ye think there'll be Elves in those trees?" Mara asked as they walked along. The grasses that spread on either side and covered the bare rock had yellowed with the season. Scraggly bushes choked the edges of the path, their leaves long since fallen, smelling of must and decay as they composted. The sky had a thin blue cast to it, the winds blowing cold across the prairies. Small rabbits sometimes bounded across the road, gathering up the last of their supplies before hibernating in deep holes for the winter.

"Don't know if they'll host Elves or not," El replied. She hadn't actually looked up where the various enclaves of the Elves might be, that they could visit, beyond the Alpine Elves high up in the mountains. She knew that Mara was more curious about them than she was.

While the other Elves were certain to be nice, kind, and welcoming, they weren't *her* people, the Ice Elves.

At some point, she and Mara would go to the frozen north. Though the journey would likely take a year, as Mara would never go on the water.

"When we get closer to the trees, I'll have a better idea," El said. "If they're all deciduous, chances are there won't be an Elf settlement. They're most likely to be holed up in evergreens."

"Ah, that makes sense. More cover to hide in," Mara said.

"Now, I've read about some of the Elven enclaves far to the east where they have a special type of tree that grows golden leaves and never loses them," El said. "But that's opposite to our home, being in the northeast portion of the Annund, while Osirholm is in the southwest portion of the land."

"Do ye want to travel there sometime?" Mara asked.

El shrugged. "While it might be pretty to see, I'm not a

Woodland Elf," she said. "If we were to embark on a long journey to see Elves, I'd much rather go home for a while."

"Home, eh?" Mara teased.

"It was where I grew up," El said, feeling slightly defensive. "Maybe a better term would be my childhood home."

She threw a quick glance over her shoulder at Mara, who gave her a warm smile. "Aye, that makes sense. Zaharbun was where I was born. I want te show ye the hearth I came from," she said.

"I'd like that," El said. She didn't like to think about how Mara had been carved inexpertly out of the flames.

Then again, if Thatur hadn't messed up the spell, Mara would still be with him, probably in the Dwarven city itself, and not with her.

They walked through the first forest, then some more prairie lands, before reaching the edge of a second forest. They hadn't been walking slowly, but had instead, let their magic aid their steps so they moved rapidly and lightly over the road.

The edges of the trees had all lost their leaves, the colors quickly fading as they piled up on the ground between the trunks. Bare branches reached for the cloudless night sky and clicked together when the wind blew.

Mara quickly got a fire going for their camp—using her magic to dry out some fallen branches before piling them together, lighting them immediately.

El set up the rest of their camp, putting up the small tent, rolling out their blankets, getting out some bread, cheese, and ham for them to munch on for dinner.

As well as tea, of course.

El used her magic to gather enough moisture from the air to fill the kettle. As long as they weren't traveling in the desert, they wouldn't have to worry about not enough water. (Too much water, as had been the case the first few days of their travel, was a different issue.) Then she set the pot into the ready coals, knowing that Mara would keep an eye on it, so that it didn't boil dry.

They sat there in the quiet dusk, eating their dinner, listening to the night settle in around them. Owls hooted in the distance, warning others of their territory. Mice scampered through the drying leaves, here and gone again. The eyes of a fox reflected the firelight for a few moments, probably trying to decide what two foolish people were doing, camping so far from home.

"El. Someone's here," Mara said quietly after they'd finished their food and were just about to start their tea.

"Who?" El said. She listened carefully, but she didn't hear anyone moving.

Then she felt it.

A presence among the trees, though it was difficult to distinguish between the being and the trees themselves.

A Woodland Elf?

She didn't think so.

"Would ye like some tea?" Mara said after a few minutes of quietly waiting for the presence to either come closer or leave. "We've got plenty."

A quiet laugh tittered on the wind.

"What need have I for your dried leaves?" came a thin, reedy voice.

"It's a comfort, for us," Mara said. "Gives our hands something to do, to hold onto, when meeting someone new."

"It's a way to share our different worlds," El added. "To break bread together, bringing peace to our various families."

A being stepped out of the trees, close enough to the firelight that El could vaguely discern their shape.

They stood tall, possibly as high as ten feet. They were willow thin, with spindly arms and legs supporting a solid, barrel-shaped torso. Twigs and dried leaves made up their hair, sticking out at all angles. Their pointed nose took up much of their face. Large, round, brilliant green eyes stared down at them. A thin mouth stretched out in what looked like a grin. Could have been a grimace, though.

It took El a moment to place the being who'd joined them.

Not a wood nymph, no, but a tree-like creature. The Elves called them the Galorey, but she thought the Humans might name them Dryads. A young one at that, as she seemed to recall that the older ones would grow even taller.

"Ye don't want to get too close to that fire," Mara said.

The creature glanced at the fire, then back at the pair of them. "You're fire," they said, point at Mara. "And you're ice. I would know what brought you together."

"It can be a longish tale," Mara said. "Or a short one. Ye choose."

"I am Einos," the person said. "And I like listening to long tales stretching into the night."

So with Einos standing at the side of their fire, in the light but still away from the heat, Mara and El told their tale, of their pasts before they arrived in Osirholm, of discovering each other, their love of business and snow cones, as well as each other.

Einos nodded as they wound down, Mara already starting to yawn. "I've heard tell of such meetings on the winds, ere now," they said. "It is my first meeting of either of your kind."

"We aren't really from around here," Mara said with a grin.

"No, you are far from your homes," Einos said. They bowed their head a little, their approximation of a nod, as their neck appeared stiffer than other people's. In order to look to the side, they had to rotate their entire body. "I am far from my home as well."

"How did ye get here, then?" Mara asked.

El also was curious. She didn't think that the Galorey ever traveled beyond the forests of their birth.

"Blown, this way, then that," Einos said. "I was first grown in woods far to the east. The golden trees were my nursemaids and sang me to sleep. But I listened too hard to the winds, who told me to shift my roots, to walk between the plains and the mountains. I have seen many things. Learned of many peoples. Traveled for most of my young life."

"And now?" El said. "What are your plans?"

"I want to go to the far waters," Einos said. "Dip my roots in ocean opposite my home. Then I'll go back, I think. Unless there are other wonders to be seen."

"I know the Woodland Elves in Osirholm would do everything they could to make you comfortable," El assured them. "But it would not be a good journey there, to go see them, I believe." She couldn't imagine the young Galorey walking along the gravel roads of the city. They'd attract too much attention, too many coming to gawk at them as they walked along. They seemed a bit shy and young to enjoy such attention.

"I've seen enough cities," Einos said dismissively. "And I know there's the Tiriandi Desert to the east of there as well. That would be a worse crossing than a raging river."

"Aye," Mara said. "Ye'd have to be extra careful, there."

They talked just a short while longer before Mara said goodnight. She needed her sleep even more since they'd started on the road, since she'd been using her magic during the day to help her travel.

"In addition to the golden trees, the Elves used to sing me lullabies as well," Einos said, sounding shy.

"Would you like me to sing for you?" El asked. "I probably don't know the same songs as you. But I can sing what I learned as a child."

"Please," Einos said. They deliberately turned their back away from the fire, looking out onto the night, the trees swaying in an unfelt breeze before them.

So El softly sang the lullabies she knew, bringing rest and peace to both Mara and Einos, her thoughts passing into dusky haze as the night grew steep and still.

At dawn break, El realized that she was sitting and meditating next to the long cold fire. Einos was gone. In their place stood a stout walking stick, stuck deeply in the ground. It came easily to El's hand.

It wasn't magical. Not really. It still had the faintest essence of a magical residue, as she suspected it had been a piece of a magical being at one time.

The wood itself was pale and golden, like freshly cut pine. A smooth nob made up the top of it, while the bottom was stout and solid. Light grains of wood ran the length of it. El wasn't sure if she saw tiny letters running along them or not.

Maybe there was writing there. Maybe it was just her imagination. Or perhaps the words would only come clear over time.

El and Mara left the spot after breaking their fast with a few bites of dried meat and some tea, both of them stating their gratefulness for the Galorey's visit the night before.

Then they were on the road again, heading ever north, El using her new walking stick.

Chapter Eight

No one challenged them at the gates leading into the mountain and the great Dwarven city of Zaharbun. The paved road held many merchant carts, both entering and leaving the city. Mostly Dwarves, but a few Humans, and even a couple of Elves rode along.

The gates themselves were as tall as a two-story house, made from solid wood and reinforced with black iron. Typical Dwarven geometric carvings covered them. The doors were supposedly perfectly balanced, and there was a hidden mechanism that could easily close them. Every winter, during the longest night, the Dwarves shut the doors at sunset, opening them again with the coming dawn of the new year. Mara hadn't seen the ceremony, but she'd been told about it.

"The outer city holds merchants, their beasts, and the like," Mara told El, drawing her off the main road and along a smaller lane. "The inner city is mainly Dwarves. The further from the doors ye go, the smaller the spaces." She glanced at El's head. "I'm shorter than ye, and even I had to crouch sometimes."

El nodded. She hadn't really thought through the consequences of being the tallest being around in a city built for shorter folk.

At least everything seemed "normal" sized in the part of the city they initially walked through. The majority of the buildings in the neighborhoods were inns and other establishments that catered to merchants and other travelers. Magical golden lights lined the ceilings and kept the place bright.

El had grown up in ice caves, far to the north, so not having the sky above her didn't really bother her.

However, the smells were so different—an undercurrent of dirt and coal, instead of ice in the air. The houses, too, were much stouter and assembled from stone or wood that had been carted in, not carved out of ice and magically imbued with strength. El didn't really notice if it was cooler or warmer than what she'd expected. Her cantrip always kept her temperature constant. If she had to guess, she'd say that it was possibly cool and welcoming.

Mara easily led them out of the Merchant's (also known as the Big Folk's) District, through the adjoining Market Ward, and into the areas of the city that had more Dwarves. El noticed that she was suddenly the tallest person in the corridor *by far*. At least it had a high enough ceiling for her to walk upright.

"This 'ere's the Bright Ring District, where the best silver merchants live and sell their jewelry," Mara told El as they passed another (invisible to her) marker that divided one district from another.

"And which district are we going to?" El asked. The great Elvish city of Llaeno had neighborhoods, where artisans were intermixed and didn't have their own special areas. Osirholm was a tiered city, and while there were some special neighborhoods on the various tiers, mostly people and the various crafts intermingled.

"Eh, first we have to go through the Crystal Borough, then the Beggar's Market, past Tower Town, afore we get to the Machinist's Palace. That's where Thatur's family lives," Mara said. "We're kinda goin' the long way round. So's I can show ye the city."

"Thank you," El said. Was Mara nervous? "Are you okay?" she asked quietly after they'd passed through more streets with what looked like regular two-story buildings with lots of apartments for families.

"I am, lass," Mara said after a moment. She reached out a warm hand and squeezed El's with it. "It's not hard to be here. Taint easy, either."

"I'm here for you, whatever you need," El said.

"I know. And it was a good idea for me to come back. To see, with new eyes," Mara said. "I wasn't really meself when I was first here."

"What's different?" El asked.

"The lights are warmer, now," Mara said instantly. "I know, it's a funny thing. But I was fighting with 'em, before. Or something like that. Now, I know they're just here, just to light the way. Not to get in the way of me own light."

El wasn't sure she completely understood, but she nodded anyway. "What else?"

"Ach, ye wouldn't have known it, but I was much more shy, then," Mara said. "Brand new born, not fully anything, and Thatur weak and sick. Scared of me own shadow, I was. So walking now, with purpose, and not being afraid to look around. That's different." Mara paused as she thought. "The houses and buildings and people look the same. They haven't changed. But *I* have. And that makes it all new."

El nodded and squeezed Mara's hand. "I get it," she said. She suspected that when they went back up north to her childhood home, she would have a similar reaction.

They wandered through Zaharbun, marveling at amazing buildings grown from crystals, laughing at the jugglers in the Beggar's Market (which turned out to be full of entertainers who "begged" for money), wandering through the huge open area that was filled with three-story tall pedestals each bearing a different clan crest, before finally getting into a neighborhood that even El recognized was different.

Instead of the geometric carvings that had predominantly been used as decorations, clockwork and gears abruptly started adorning the buildings, outlining windows, doors, balconies, and arches. The air held the smell of machine oil. A low purring noise underlay the gruff conversations of Dwarves and the calls of the merchants. The ceiling encroached on them, and El found herself having to duck her head now and again.

Finally, Mara led them down a narrow lane. The houses here were all two stories, tall and proud, the black and gray stone decorated with silver and gold gears, wheels, and other machinery.

"This is it," she said, stopping at a bright door painted the same color red as Nilafels.

"I'm right here with you," El said. She gave Mara a quick hug.

Snalgrud said they should visit.

Hopefully the rest of the family would be as understanding.

❋

Fortunately, the family turned out to have a "tall room" as they referred to it, where they could put El and Mara, so the Elf could stand up straight at night.

The rest of the family, well, they were very typical for Dwarves. Hard-working. Gruff. They gave secret smiles to El and Mara when they thought no one else was looking.

Durikkuth Icemaster, Thatur's grandmother, insisted that they call her Duri. Though she was not young, her face heavily wrinkled and her hands no longer strong enough to wield a hammer, she had a warmth to her that reminded El of bright summer sunshine.

The rest of the family was welcoming enough. For Dwarves. El was an Elf, and they were historically enemies, though there hadn't been wars between their peoples for centuries. However, they were both long-lived folk, and had memories that went deep.

They were welcomed and feasted heavily that first day, though neither El or Mara could truly appreciate the dishes, eating lightly enough that Duri and the others teased them about wasting away.

That night, before they went back to the room they'd been given, Mara brought El to what had been Thatur's workshop.

Other Dwarves now worked there, producing the magical parts that went into the Dwarven war machines.

On one side, three workbenches were lined up. Each had its own personality: one completely neat and tidy, one strewn with gears and other metallic bits and bobs, and one with spellbooks piled high.

But that was only half the room. The other half was dominated by a large hearth that took up most of the wall. A stone mantel ran across the top of it. The hearth was nearly as tall as

El, made of rough, dark brown brick. A black iron bar had been implanted on one side, with an arm that swung in over the flames and out again. Beside it, a kettle for water sat.

The fire had been banked, so just coals glowed in the dim lights.

Mara reached out and touched the mantel, running her fingers over it, before turning to El. "This is me hearth," she said softly. "Thatur had it built special for his workshop." She paused, dipping her head under the arch of the fireplace. "It's been cleaned up, some. Was black when I stepped out. Been burning so hot and hard."

El merely nodded. She wanted to reach out and hold Mara's hand, but it wasn't time. Not yet.

Mara examined the base of the hearth for a moment before she pointed to a cracked brick. "There," she said softly. "I took me first step. Came out of the fire so hungry, trying to burn everything I touched, to keep that glut of magic flowing toward me."

El did reach out now, resting one hand on Mara's shoulder.

The fire elemental took a deep breath and shook her head. "I didn't mean to," she said.

"I know. The family knows. You didn't know any better," El said.

Mara turned toward her silently.

El wrapped her arms around the sobbing elemental, trying to bring what comfort she could. It surprised her how cool Mara was, her grief dampening her essential warmth.

When they finally made it back to their room, Mara's fires were burning bright again. El stayed awake all night, holding her partner, stroking her skin when the nightmares made her tremble.

By morning, Mara was calm again, the storm weathered.

El knew there would be more tears, but she felt as though some of that initial grief was finally healing, particularly when the Dwarves all welcomed them at breakfast and still seemed happy to see them.

Mara's tears were gone. For now.

Chapter Nine

Though they'd asked as soon as they arrived, they couldn't meet with the Dwarven elders of the Icemaster clan for two days. As far as El understood, though many of the Dwarves that shared the name Icemaster could be considered blood, that is, family, there were so many branches (twigs, sticks, and possibly forests) of relatives that *clan* was the more correct title.

The meeting was held in one of the local Dwarven temples, dedicated to Rutaburra, the local God of War. (Since many of the creations by the Icemaster clan were the Dwarven siege machines used by the Elves to fight the ice demons, the family had officially changed their affiliation from the God of the Forge to the God of War.)

The temple was cold enough that El noticed it before her cantrip kicked in to warm her. Statues of massive, two-story-tall heroes lined the long hallway they walked down, toward the collection of elders waiting for them at the altar. The statues were all Dwarven warriors, carved with hard faces and bearing mighty axes, swords, and shields. There was even one with a bow, which surprised El.

The lights here were distant and many shadows gathered at the feet of the frozen warriors as they walked. It sort of reminded El of Azutjengaban's entrance hall, lined with all the ice statues of people who the Dragon thought were pretty, though the eyes of the Dwarven statues were more alive. Dust motes danced in what few lights there were, and floral incense threaded through the air.

Two dozen elders had gathered that day, ready to hear Mara's request. She wasn't really a Dwarf. There wasn't a technical need for her to get their permission to marry anyone. However, according to Duri, they'd found her request respectful and had decided to honor it.

Both El and Mara wore clothing that was more Dwarven in appearance. Instead of her usual long off-white robes, El wore a loose blouse under a tightly fitting, heavily embroidered sky-blue vest. The embroidery was all done in white thread, patterns of leaves and flowers, a nod to her "Elfyness" as Duri had proclaimed when presenting the clothes to her. She also wore thick black trousers that ended just past her knee, though she kept her own soft black-leather boots that had brought her so far. Usually, El wore her long chestnut-brown hair down, but today, it had been bound up in Dwarven braids, adorned with small machine cogs and tiny hammers.

Mara wore a tunic as usual, this time, though, with a blouse underneath. The tunic had also been provided by Duri, a rich brown with a subtle, geometric pattern of dark red flames embroidered on it. Her golden skin glowed in the dim light. El found herself staring, captured by her partner's warmth.

"Welcome, Mara Fane, and your chosen partner, Elbriarien Itamar, as well," called out a large Dwarf standing at the center of the elders. "I am Nurandubo, current leader of the Icemaster clan." He wore a magnificently embroidered vest, covered in gold and silver thread. The other elders wore similarly extravagant outfits, including one Dwarf with a red-and-white striped top hat that made him almost as tall as El.

El and Mara both bowed appropriately low, particularly given their larger stature.

"Though yer not a Dwarf, nor have ye been adopted by the Icemaster clan, we understand that ye want to pay your respects and ask permission to marry this one. Who is also not a Dwarf," Nurandubo continued.

El hid her smile, understanding that the elders had fewer problems with Mara marrying but did have more concerns given that she was an Elf.

"I was created by Thatur Icemaster," Mara said. "Drawn from the hearth by him. The Dwarves are me family. I wanna do right by them, follow their customs."

This had all been cleared ahead of time, Duri instructing them on what to say.

"Yer a mistake," came a reedy voice from the back. "Almost a great one."

A darker skinned Dwarf pushed his way to the front. He glared at them from under bushy eyebrows. His shirt and vest were just as finely made as the other elders, but El felt as though shadows clung to him.

"Thatur Icemaster paid for his mistake with his life," Mara said softly. "I know what happened. What he did, and what I did." She sounded so sad, El wanted to reach out and wrap her arms around her. However, she held herself stiffly apart, not wanting to accidentally bring disgrace to either of them.

"You. Elf," the new Dwarf said. "Ye know what happens when ye use magic too strong. Yer peoples still fighting the Great Mistake five centuries later. Why should we reward someone who could have brought down the same terror on us all? Fire demons roaming the halls of this mountain, destroying our homes and hard work."

El saw more than one Dwarf shudder at the image.

It would have been a disaster if even one had slipped through.

"But Thatur Icemaster was a true Mage," Mara pointed out. "He took the damage into himself, rather than set it loose in the world."

"Yer still a mistake," this shadowy Dwarf insisted. "Thatur was reaching too far."

Nurandubo stepped in at this point. "Garrig, yer a great Mage. Thatur was trying to follow yer footsteps."

"And he failed," Garrig pointed out. Again. "Created this broken—thing."

El bristled at that. Mara was no *thing*. She was a person in her own right.

Before she could step up to defend her partner, Mara spoke.

"Aye, I wasn't whole, not when I stepped from me hearth," she said softly. "But iffen yer such a great Mage, surely ye can see that I've changed?"

"That's beside the point," Garrig said dismissively.

"No, tis the *entire* point," Mara said. "When a fire demon threatened to destroy the city of Osirholm, Elbriarien and I defeated it. El, by adapting her ice spells to bring rain. Me, by absorbing all its fire."

Suddenly, Mara started to glow, outlined by ghostly, flickering flames.

"I'm not that broken creature. Not no more. I'm a full fire elemental, in me own right," she added, taking a step forward.

El sensed that Garrig wanted to deny Mara's claims. However, a different Dwarf stepped forward now. She was one of the younger Dwarves there, her hair and beard still solidly brown with no grey. She wore a black vest, black shirt, and black pants. However, they were all heavily embroidered with gold thread.

It took El a moment to realize that like Mara's tunic, the designs were all stylized flames.

"A full fire elemental! How fortuitous!" she exclaimed. "I'm Arakread, Mistress of the great forge Nithouc. You must come to visit!"

El blinked, surprised. Though it made sense, that if the Icemaster clan made Dwarven siege engines, they'd need to forge the metal for their machines, and not just be focused on the ice magic that they used.

"Are you truly a full elemental, now?" Nurandubo asked, sounding both cautious and curious.

"I am," Mara said proudly, stepping back and dousing her flames. "And I mean to marry me partner, a full Ice Elf."

That brought some quiet murmuring amongst the elders.

"Elbriarien, you control ice?" Nurandubo said.

"I do," El said, stepping forward herself now. She held up her wrist to show her Mage Mark. "I grew up in the far north. Used the great Dwarven war machines to fight ice demons. They truly are a marvel," she added.

"Fire. And Ice," Nurandubo proclaimed. "The elements that Thatur Icemaster sought to conquer himself. I think ye'd make yer master proud, with this union."

El kept her expression grave (*not* snooty, as Duri had teased her more than once). Still, she felt her heart lighten.

"Are ye through with yer objections and yer grandstanding?" Nurandubo said, looking directly at Garrig.

The shadowy Dwarf glared at Nurandubo, but after a few moments, gave a curt nod.

"Does anyone else have something they want to say?" Nurandubo asked of the rest of the elders.

None of them said anything, though El did notice that more of them were giving her speculative looks.

"Then we, the elders of the Icemaster clan, do give ye our blessing," Nurandubo announced.

"Thank ye," Mara said. She bowed low to the group.

El joined her, happy that Mara had been granted her wish.

As soon as they straightened back up, the elders all stepped forward. They split into three groups: one group who nodded as they passed, leaving the temple, one group who clustered around Mara and peppered her with questions about fire, and the last who came to ask El questions about ice.

El glanced over at Mara at one point, only to receive a huge grin in return.

These were her people, in many ways. And they seemed to have finally not just accepted her, but seen her worth.

Though they'd planned on leaving Zaharbun in just a few days, it appeared that they'd be there for a while yet, given how many Dwarves had invited them to come to their workshops.

It would be worth it.

Chapter Ten

It was the day before El and Mara would finally get on the road again, traveling back to Osirholm. They'd been there for two full weeks, meeting with various Dwarven masters, working with them on either fire or ice magic. As a result, they'd planned on heading straight back to Osirholm, and not making the trip up the mountain to visit any of the Alpine Elves.

Though the Icemaster family had wanted to arrange for transportation back for them, El and Mara had refused. They could actually make better time if they used their magic while they traveled, going much further in a normal day than a cart would.

And they did have to get back to Osirholm. They had a business to run, which all of the Dwarves understood and appreciated.

That afternoon, they were having tea with Duri in her sitting room. The place was small and cramped. Neither El or Mara could fully stand. Knickknacks covered every available horizontal surface, while artwork, carvings, and portraits filled the walls. (Not that all that made El claustrophobic. Much.)

The small, overstuffed couch took up one wall, and two wooden rockers faced it. A pot-bellied stove warmed the room from the corner. The air smelled of lavender and machine oil, a strange combination.

El and Mara both elected to sit on the floor, which was actually the perfect height for them to reach the table that held the teapot and the tray of delectable pastries.

"Eh, it's been a good visit, yes?" Duri asked them after they'd all served themselves.

"It has been," Mara said with some satisfaction.

El nodded. She felt as though the Icemaster clan had come to appreciate both of them for their varied skills and magic.

They'd also created iced treats for the family more than one evening for dessert. Mara had worked with the family's cook to develop the syrups, while El had provided the ice. Seemed that Snalgrud had come back with stories about the treats and everyone had wanted to try them.

"I'm glad ye came," Duri said. "Particularly to put that nasty Garrig in his place."

"What's his story?" Mara asked. "He seemed so resentful of me."

"Yer not wrong," Duri said, nodding. "As ye know, Thatur never married. Too dedicated to learning his craft, studying magic."

El drew back her presence, trying to make herself less visible. It was a cantrip all Elves had, though it worked best when they were in their own environment. A Woodland Elf couldn't be found among the trees if they didn't want to. Same with an Ice Elf in the snow.

This was a moment between Duri and Mara. She was just sharing it, an outsider, looking in.

"He was one of the youngest Ice Mages we had," Duri

continued, sounding proud. "But that weren't good enough. He wanted more. Like Garrig, he wanted to be a stronger, more powerful Mage."

"Garrig's magic—it isn't merely ice, is it?" Mara said. "He has another skill."

Duri barked an unkind laugh. "No, taint just ice. See, Thatur was going to do one better than Garrig. That boy became an Ice Mage, then went on to Smoke Mage. It's a strange sort of combination of fire and ice. 'E couldn't get to a full Fire Mage. Had to stop."

Huh. El hadn't ever heard of a Smoke Mage. Were there also Mist Mages as well as Dust or Ash Mages? Elements that weren't as pure as fire, water, earth or air?

She'd have to check in the library at the Elven enclave when they got back home.

"They were always in competition, those two," Duri said softly. "So while the family didn't blame ye for Thatur's death, there's some who do blame Garrig, for spurring Thatur on."

Mara tilted her head to the side. "That doesn't seem right, though," she said. "He didn't make Thatur chose to try fire magic. He didn't steal Thatur's life from him."

"Now, none of that," Duri chided. "Garrig did flaunt his powers when he could. He and Thatur were close. Not brothers, but we all wondered iffen they'd been lovers, once upon a time."

Mara just nodded and didn't seem surprised by that. "Thatur only mentioned Garrig once, at the very end, just before he died. Saying he was sorry they hadn't parted on better terms."

"Aye," Duri said. "They was squabbling a lot during the weeks afore he tried to carve you from the hearth." She shook her head. "So while Garrig might publicly blame you for his death, I'm thinking he blames himself, too."

Mara dropped her head and studied her teacup.

El reached out and put her hand on Mara's back, to remind her that she wasn't alone, that she was loved and would be cherished for the rest of her days.

After a few moments of them all sitting quietly, Duri asked, "So when are ye getting married?"

"We haven't picked a date yet," El said smoothly. She and Mara hadn't talked about the wedding while they'd been in the Dwarven city. She hoped that now that Mara had gotten permission from the Icemaster elders that she'd want to move forward more quickly.

"Eh, ye just let us know. Someone will be there," Duri assured them.

"Thank you," Mara said, finally looking up from her teacup and giving them both a wobbly smile.

"So what are some Dwarven traditions, when it comes to getting married?" El asked. Though she'd planned on speaking with Brytha about Dwarven customs, she'd never found the time during the busy summer months.

"It starts with the promenade," Duri said solemnly. "The one who proposed, their family, friends, and maybe clan elders, depending, gather and have a grand breakfast feast, with quite a few toasts and bragging along with it. Then they march through the districts, to the house of their proposed one. When they get there, usually all of the other's family has also gathered for a breakfast feast. More toasts are given, and the entire group then marches to the temple to get married."

"Which temple?" Mara asked.

"Eh, depends on the clan. Most use the temple of the Earth Goddess, the one who also oversees the mines. Kurithi. Sometimes, though, they'll use the temple of Kiritum, the God of Commerce," Duri said.

That made sense. Dwarves were well known for their bargaining techniques and business sense.

"The priestess or priest gives 'em a quick blessing. Then joins the group as they continue their promenade through the districts, buying drinks at every tavern they stumble across," Duri concluded.

"We've seen a couple of wedding parties come through the shop," Mara said.

"Aye. Ye need yer strength, and to refuel, 'cause sometimes the drinking lasts for three days, everyone wanting to give a toast and bring cheer to the married couple," Duri said. "Plus, while everyone is there at the party, the couple can't sneak off and enjoy themselves. They have to be there the whole time. Families sometimes have it planned out, with one group taking over when some of the first group loses steam, so the toasting and drinking can go on for longer." She gave a soft smile. "Me own wedding, we lasted for four full days afore we had to call it quits."

El shook her head. She wasn't sure she wanted to do something like that, have a party throughout all of Osirholm that lasted for days. Mara, she knew, wouldn't be able to last that long. She needed sleep like a Human.

But if Mara was determined to do it, El would be there, by her side.

Chapter Eleven

El and Mara increased their magical speed while on the road going back to Osirholm. El's walking stick helped her, making her feel even less tired by night. Traveling so fast meant that they spent more nights camping along the path, as the inns weren't spaced out to accommodate such speed.

It was worth it, though, when they reached the flatter lands and the scrubby bushes and trees. El felt her soul lighten at the sight.

They agreed to slow down slightly at that point. They didn't want to arrive in Osirholm in the middle of the night. They'd spend one last night on the road, then get to the city midday.

Though it had rained for most of the day—a fine drizzle more similar to a heavy mist than proper drops—by evening, the sky had cleared and they could see the stars.

They had their camp set up quickly, dinner and tea made and consumed, as the night deepened. In the distance, mice scurried and rustled between the dried-out bushes. A fox yipped its joy, probably having found its dinner. The air smelled of the nearby sagebrush and the small puddles that gathered around them.

El stayed quiet, willing to give Mara the time and space to speak. She had the feeling that Mara had something to say, and she didn't want to make her partner feel rushed.

"Eh—it's been a good journey," Mara eventually said. "I'm glad we went to see the Icemasters."

"I am as well," El said. "Even though I'm afraid that Arakread is going to camp out at our doorstep some year, just to get you to light her forge every day."

Mara snorted.

The Forge Mistress had been the most persistently curious about all of Mara's different flames, as well as the various applications of them in her craft. The others had eventually stopped pestering Mara with questions, while Arakread kept coming up with more and different things she'd wanted a fire elemental to try.

"Did you get what you needed?" El finally asked quietly.

Mara gave a sigh that even El could feel at the bottom of her heart.

"Yes. And no," she said. "I got the blessing of the elders. That means something to me." She paused, then speared El with a glance. "Though ye know I would have married ye even if they'd withheld it, right?"

El shrugged. "I'm glad it didn't come down to that."

Mara peered at her, but El didn't comment further.

Sure, Mara said that. And she probably would have followed through on her word. However, it also would have bothered her, and that tiny grain of sand, of friction, didn't always develop into something beautiful, like a pearl.

"But." Mara paused. Took a deep breath. Sighed again.

"But I still don't have a good idea what we'll do for a ceremony."

"That's something we get to figure out," El said, trying to sound brighter and happier than she felt. "We get to determine what works for us. Which traditions we want to follow. Or invent."

Mara nodded and didn't say anything.

El kept her own sigh silent. She wasn't sure what to say to bring Mara comfort.

Making up a tradition didn't make it a tradition. "First annual" was a phrase that Wyne had taught them in business and Mara hated using.

However, their relationship wasn't a business. It wasn't something that either of them took lightly.

How could she give Mara the formality of a true tradition? Yet still have it be unique and work for them?

El went to spend time with Nel later that week. Both she and Mara took time away from the shop, and each other. While they loved each other, they needed time alone as well.

She hadn't spent a lot of time with Nel just before they'd left—they were both so busy with their own businesses.

However, the inn wasn't as full during the rainy season, though the tavern would be just as packed later that evening.

"Welcome back!" Nel called when El stepped in. The tavern had just opened, and El had managed to arrive before any customers.

"Thank you," El said, coming to sit at the bar. The room smelled of honeyed mead and sour ale. The fire burned cheerily in the hearth, bringing not just warmth but light to the room. She always felt comfortable here.

"I take it you were successful?" Nel said as she started sorting out some tea for them.

El sighed. "Partially," she said, telling Nel the truth.

The Dwarves had accepted them, and given their blessing.

However, that wasn't enough for Mara. El planned on doing more research that week, going to the library to find different Elven traditions that might work for them.

Nel served them both some tea and listened, then was quiet for a few moments afterward.

"I didn't want to mention it before, but my cousin's back in town," Nel said.

"Oh?" El asked politely. She had no idea why Nel thought that was significant.

Nel sighed. "Lanador's a handful. He's young. And careless."

Careless was never good, at least among the Elves. El waited while Nel gathered her thoughts.

"He's also one of the best guides you can get through the Tiriandi Desert," Nel added all in a rush. She stopped and looked expectantly at El.

"And why would I want to go through the desert? What's there?" El had to ask.

"Lanador claims he's stumbled across the home of a fire elemental," Nel said. "I didn't believe him at first. No one did. Why would a fire elemental make their home in the most desolate area of the desert? Nothing grows there. It's just sand and dry."

"But you believe him now?" El asked warily.

"He's found something, far out over the sands," Nel said. "There are heated vents in the area, places where the earth grows thin and fire lies directly underneath. He swears that some sort of being has carved out an area for themselves there. He claims he walked through a grove of glass statues." Nel grimaced. "At least he wasn't stupid enough to try to steal anything. He did sketch out a few of the images. And that was what convinced me, as well as most of my family, that he had actually found something in the desert. He might be careless, and young enough to be clueless, but he isn't creative enough to make up something like this."

Nel reached under the bar, cursed, then spent a few more moments shuffling through papers.

"Here," Nel said, sliding two folded pieces of paper across to El. "What do you think?"

El carefully unfolded the marked and stained papers. The first had a simple pencil sketch of a thin figure that looked like a willowy woman, except that it appeared to be blown out of three intertwining tubes of glass that each ended in a flame. It was very abstract, yet El couldn't see any shape other than a woman in it.

The second figure was more squat with harder edges, but still nothing square. It mostly resembled a table, though one that had an empty spot in the center of it, and three spindly legs that looked organically grown out of glass, not shaped. It almost had a crystalline structure to it.

"Huh," El said. "Can I show these to Mara? See what she thinks of them?"

"Please, do," Nel said. "I don't know if I should believe Lanador or not. But if you decide to go with him, he will take care of you in the desert. He is a good guide, despite everything else."

"Thank you," El said seriously.

If Mara could meet and talk with another fire elemental,

that might go a long ways toward the pair of them figuring out what they wanted to do for their own marriage ceremony.

"I meant to tell you this ages ago," Nel confessed. "But Lanador didn't have the sketches at that point, so it was more a rumor than anything else."

"It's all right," El said. "We had to go see the Dwarves first, to get their blessing, before we did anything else."

El left soon after that, hurrying back to the shop.

Had she finally found the key for Mara?

Chapter Twelve

Later that evening, the pair of them sat in their bedroom. El sat in the chair that Mara had bought for her, while Mara sprawled on the bed, looking at first one sketch, then the other, then back again.

Finally, she sat up and faced El.

"I don't know if those figures have been created by a fire elemental or not," she said slowly. "I'm guessing too much. Maybe I want it too much." She reached out and touched one of the drawings, sliding gentle fingers across the sketch. "What I can say is that something about these sings to me heart. There's the grace of fire to them."

El nodded, trying not to be too excited about the prospect.

"So do you want to try to make a trip across the Tiriandi Desert?" she asked. "To try to find this creator?"

"I do," Mara said. She gave El a soft, sad smile. "I know you want to get married. To put on those pretty red promise bracelets, and maybe go sip some dew together."

El just grinned at her. Duri had teased them about Elvish customs, such as sipping the freshest dew from the field.

(Which, okay, perhaps the Woodland or the Alpine Elves did such things. Ice Elves did *not*.)

(They may have had some customs involving catching the first snowflakes of winter on your tongue, but that wasn't the same thing at all.)

(Really.)

"And I know ye plan on doing some more research, finding magic for us to try. But this...I think this is our best bet. Finding someone who might be like me."

El reached out and took one of Mara's perpetually warm hands in hers. "Are you lonely?" she had to ask.

"Eh, I don't know," Mara said, shaking her head. "I don't think it's that. Or just that. Yer far from yer people. Do you get lonely for yer kin?"

"Sometimes," El admitted, though she'd never been that close to her family. "I do miss the fresh cold of a winter day. The bright blue skies over the white hills. The hush that comes with the first snow. I love it here. Still..."

"Aye," Mara said. "I know what you mean. I don't want to lose you. The shop. The little ones and all their bright, brilliant ideas. But the thought of finding another of me kind, to ask about meself...it's too good to pass up."

"I understand," El said. "I'll talk with Nel, set up a meeting with this Lanador. It's still the rainy season. It's a good time for us to go travel for a bit again, before it gets warm."

"Thank you," Mara said. "I'm so grateful for ye, and the acceptance ye bring to me life."

Then she went ahead and proved that gratitude, while El tried to make sure Mara understood just how much she, too, was loved.

❆

Lanador, like Nel, was an Umber Elf, with brilliantly white hair that stuck out all over his head, black skin, and red eyes.

He was also taller than both of them, standing at least six foot seven. He looked long and drawn out, with a sharp nose, lanky limbs, and a skinny torso. He sprawled rather than sat in a chair at *The Book Ends* inn the next night, when El and Mara came to see him.

He looked at them curiously as they came up to the table, his red eyes darting between them.

"There isn't much water in the desert," he started off with, rather than introductions. "I don't know how the likes of you will fare," he added, nodding toward El.

She shrugged, glanced over at Mara, who nodded. They sat and got right to business.

"I'll have to carry water," El said softly. "I figure that will make up most of my pack."

Lanador nodded. "I can find water in the desert. When there's any to be found," he added. "But it's going to be harder than you think."

Then he turned his attention to Mara. "And you're a fire elemental?"

"I am," Mara said. "I'd like to meet another of me kind."

Lanador looked a little uncomfortable at that. "My cousin Neladrie's been harping on me about that. See, I never saw the person who created those statues. I just think they're a fire elemental. I can't tell you why."

Mara nodded. "I understand that. The being who created these..." she paused and pulled out the drawings that Lanador had made, "...this person knows fire. I can see the flame shapes in them."

"See! I knew it!" Lanador exclaimed. He suddenly sat up and look a lot more excited.

And young. Oh, so young. It made El's heart ache when she realized just how young this Elf was.

"There's fire in them. I know it," Lanador said, nodding. "And it makes sense that it's some sort of fire creature out there, in the heart of the desert. There isn't anything else around. Sure, there are lizards and scorpions and such. You won't starve," he assured the pair of them. "But there just isn't a lot of anything there. Just sand."

"I don't need to eat a lot," Mara said. "I look better, more like a person when I do. But the flames and heat will sustain me for quite some time."

El nodded. While she didn't need that much to eat either, Mara needed less. It was one of the ways they balanced each other out—Mara needed more sleep, El needed more food. Not as much as a Human, of course. But she couldn't live just on tea.

"Are you ready to go tomorrow then? Crack of dawn?" Lanador asked excitedly.

"Uhm, we have a business to run. And we've just come back from a long trip. We'll be ready to go..." El turned to look at Mara, who shrugged at her, leaving the planning up to her.

"How about three days from now? On the rest day?"

"All right. Fine," Lanador said with an expressive sigh.

El didn't give him the grin she wanted to. He sounded like Sigder when being asked to do a math problem.

"But we do want to go sooner rather than later," Lanador warned. "It's the cool season. It will be much easier to pass across the sands at this point."

"Will we be traveling during the day? Or at night?" El asked. From the few accounts she'd read about the desert, even the Elves did most of their travel at night.

"Some of each," Lanador said. "At the start, we can travel

with the sun. As we get closer to the center of the desert, it's hotter. We'll need to start traveling at night, then, probably one or two days out from our destination."

Mara grimaced, but nodded. They'd have to bring some of the tea that Nel had given El, that would wake her up.

"So, did you only approach this area at night?" El had to ask. "Where the statues were?"

"I did," Lanador said. "I didn't want to travel too far during the day."

"And you never met anyone?" Mara asked, catching what El might be asking about.

"I didn't," Lanador said. He looked from one to the other of them, seeming to understand that they might have something to add. "Why? Why is that important?"

El gave him a grin. "Mara needs to sleep at night," she said. "Don't know if that's a fire elemental thing or just a her thing. But it does make me wonder if the person we're looking for might also spend the nights sleeping."

"That doesn't make sense," Lanador said. "Most desert creatures sleep during the day. Not at night."

"They might not be a desert creature," El pointed out. "But a creature of fire."

"And fires always get banked at night," Mara continued. "I figure that's part of me sleepiness. I came from a hearth that didn't flame all the time."

El nodded. She and Mara had talked of this before.

They drew up lists of things that they would need to bring for their journey. That included some minerals that other artisans used to color glass, that they would bring as a gift for the being.

Lanador insisted that El's pack be only half-full, as he'd be expecting her to carry the water jugs he'd provide after they were on their way. As an Umber Elf, he didn't need as much water. Mara, she suspected, didn't need much either.

However, though she would be the most affected by the desert and the heat, she still felt it was important that she go on this journey. Particularly if she'd have the opportunity to meet another fire elemental.

She just had to survive until then.

It wasn't going to be that difficult, was it?

Chapter Thirteen

Though Lanador complained, El and Mara both insisted on taking the "long" route into Tiriandi. Instead of heading there directly, they went along the regular trade route for two days to reach Barithel, the closest of the Umber Elf cities. From there, they'd cut north, heading into the desert.

While they understood his desire for a quicker, shorter route, both El and Mara were excited to experience an Elven city.

The landscape changed gradually as they walked, starting with the familiar scraggly bare bushes and yellowish stones, transitioning to cactus and the occasional scrub tree. The earth grew more reddish brown and the stones that dared raise their heads to the burning skies had been bleached white. Rain had followed them. For several hours both afternoons, torrential downpours drenched them, making their progress even slower along muddy roads. El did feel more confident than the others, given her walking stick, but when she suggested to Mara that she could use it, the fire elemental turned her down vehemently.

Appeared that the stick didn't like her fire magic, and always felt prickly when she touched it.

Eventually, the rains stopped and the skies cleared late afternoon of the second day. They paused at the top of a hillside. Lanador pointed to the white spot in the distance. "That's Barithel," he told them. It was already late afternoon, and the rain had just stopped. "We'll make it there late evening if we hurry."

El and Mara both nodded. They'd only been using their magic to speed their steps when they could see clearly. Now, they raced down the slope toward the bright lights.

Houses made from brown brick started to line the road as they neared the city. They were all one-story, squat, and poorly maintained. Mara shot El a questioning look.

"Not Elves," she said. "Probably Humans."

"Nope," Lanador said with a grin. "Gnomes."

That surprised El. She would have thought that they'd take better care of their dwellings.

Lanador took them down a side road, toward a taller building, the only one with two stories in the area. It, too, looked dingy and practically falling apart.

"Look for the magic," he told the pair of them.

El was one of the few Elves she knew who could see magic, so she was surprised when Lanador asked them to do that. Was it a more common ability among the Umber Elves?

From Mara's gasp, she knew that something was up.

The building in front of them was *not* tumbling in on itself. No, there were magical buttresses, invisible until she looked for something outside the ordinary, holding up the roof. In addition, bright green magical carvings swirled on the walls, giving them a more graceful appearance.

"Look in one of the windows," Lanador instructed next.

"This is one of the Gnome temples, so you can't go in, except on the holidays."

El stepped to the side, along with Mara, and looked.

She couldn't contain her gasp.

The walls inside appeared to be completely covered in ornate gold trimmings that shone under the light of hundreds of candles. Splashes of other colors appeared randomly spaced until she realized they were all gemstones held in carefully carved settings: emeralds the size of her fist, rubies bigger than her head, turquoise shards longer than her arm, as well as other precious stones.

"The insides of all the houses around here are just as gaudy," Lanador said disapprovingly.

Astonished, El turned to Mara. "Did you know this?" she had to ask.

"I had no idea," Mara said. Then she snorted. "No wonder Vorwin calls ye beige."

El had to giggle at that. If this was what a typical Gnome settlement looked like, then yes, comparatively, she had a definite lack of color in her life.

They made their way back to the main road. El maintained her awareness of the magic held by the buildings, constantly marveling at the different designs. She was glad they were approaching as dusk drew near, as it made the magic glow brighter.

Very few Gnomes traveled along the main road. El was about to ask why when she smelled the spices and cooking food in the air. It was dinnertime for most folk. Her own stomach grumbled a little at the smell of freshly baked bread, garlicky potatoes, roasted lamb, and maybe even some sort of berry compote.

"Mmm," Mara said. "I hope yer Elves are gonna give me a dinner as good as this smells."

El glanced at her, worried.

Mara gave her a reassuring grin. "I know, I know. Cold pickled vegetables are all I'm a likely to get."

Lanador seemed offended. "Of course we can put on a feast that will outshine any of the Gnome cooks."

El snorted, but didn't comment. Elves didn't eat as much. Their food tended to be beautiful but their portions, small.

At least Nel seemed to prefer smokier flavors, which Mara favored as well.

They'd just have to wait and see.

White stone walls ringed the actual city of Barithel, though no one appeared to be manning the gates, no guards questioning people as they went in and out.

The walls themselves stood at least two stories tall. The crenelation was made up of pointed, leaf-like pieces, not flat and broad. El assumed that a walkway ran behind them.

No decorations, magical or otherwise, adorned the white walls. The starkness was its own sort of beauty, though.

Huge iron doors lay flat against the tunnel going through the wall. It gave El an appreciation for how thick the walls were: at least six feet wide at this entrance point. The doors had many small scenes done in bas-relief, showing Elves planting crops, herding animals, working with Dwarves to mine for stone, and so on. Pictures of war dominated the bottom of the decorations, showing Elves shooting arrows from the city walls to decimate the monsters gathered before them.

When Mara asked about the war scenes, Lanador explained

that about a century before, a magical spell had gone awry, and the Elves had had to fight off an invasion of fire demons. It hadn't lasted as long as the Great Mistake—there had just been the one incursion. El figured that was the reason why she'd never heard of it before.

Then again, magical mistakes happened. Not all were worth noting.

Mara reached out and squeezed El's hand as she stood there for a moment, pondering.

Some year, her people would be free of their own Great Mistake. All their resources would no longer go to fighting the ice demons.

What could they build?

Chapter Fourteen

Stepping beyond the walls and into the city made El's breath catch.

Twilight was upon them, a time that all Elves felt was sacred, that transition time that was neither day nor night. White buildings rose up before her, softly glowing even in the dimness. Magical blue lights twinkled from the tops of carved columns that lined the road. A soft flute trilled in the distance, a song welcoming the coming moon. The scent of cooking fires and heavenly spices filled the air, making her mouth water.

El reached out and squeezed Mara's hand as they walked forward. A few Elves looked curiously at them as they passed. Everyone wore the same sorts of clothes that Nel wore—sleeveless tunics with pants and sandals. More than one of the Elves they passed had their ears pierced with many gold rings, like Nel.

They were all Umber Elves, with black skin that made it easy for them to blend into the shadows. Even with their white hair, they still looked like part of the night.

El knew that she must stick out quite a bit, her own skin as pale as freshly fallen snow. Mara did as well, with her warm golden skin and auburn hair.

Lanador led them straight to an inn, just a few blocks from the gates, called *The Hidden Garden*. While the walls looked the same as the rest of the nearby buildings—white, unadorned, and slightly glowing—the door was painted a bright red and had silver filigreed decorations across it.

El found her breath catching again as she walked in. Instead of chairs and tables, everyone sat on colorful rugs and cushions on the ground. Small, square depressions had been dug into the floor, so people could sit on the edge with feet in the hole. Along the walls of the room, she finally saw a few tall tables that people could stand around, though they were all empty at this point.

The room looked cozier than she'd been expecting. Then again, Ice Elves didn't sit on the floor. It was likely to not merely be cold, but frequently wet as well.

All along the right side of the room ran the bar. The legs of the bar looked precariously put together out of yellow, brown, and white field stones, though El suspected that strong magic held it together. A solid piece of black slate covered the top of it. A huge hearth took up most of the left wall, tall enough for an Elf to stand in. The cheery fire gave the room a warm glow, along with the magical golden lights glittering near the ceiling.

Most of the people they passed by on their way to the bar were Umber Elves, though El did see a couple of Gnomes in one of the corners. A Human stood behind the bar, though.

"What'll it be?" he asked jovially.

Unlike most of the Humans that El interacted with in Osirholm, this man stood almost as tall as her. Muscles bunched across his shoulders, making him seem slightly stooped. He'd broken his nose at some point and he hadn't bothered seeing a healer to fix it, so it looked squashed and overly large, taking up a good portion of his reddish face. Clear gray eyes twinkled at them under bushy white-haired eyebrows, while his bald skull reflected the lights in the room.

"Two rooms, and dinner for three," Lanador said. They haggled a bit on the price, which El was grateful for. They were paying for all of their accommodations as part of their agreement of hiring Lanador as their guide.

It turned out the rooms were all upstairs. The inn keeper—Taimund, though he went by just Tai—instructed them to go wash up and they'd have food ready soon.

The rooms upstairs were organized in a square. Mara and El had a corner room that was slightly bigger than the mere closet that Lanador had. He appeared to be expecting it, though, and so wasn't upset. The room reminded El of where she'd stayed when she'd first arrived in Osirholm, with a cool, red-tile floor, brightly painted yellow walls, a washstand in the corner and a small curtained off area for packs to be stashed.

When they stepped back out into the hall, they found Lanador waiting for them. "Notice anything unusual about the layout here?" he asked.

El and Mara looked at each other, then shrugged.

"Take a look around," Lanador instructed.

El walked one way down the hall while Mara walked the other way. When they met up close to the staircase, El finally realized what Lanador wanted them to see.

"The doorways are all on one side of the hallway, against the outer wall," she said. "This space, here," she continued, indicating the other side, "has no obvious doors in it." Swathes of colorful cloth hung from the ceiling, covering the inner walls like drapes.

Lanador grinned at her. "That's it exactly. Now, where's the magic?" he asked.

Mara replied. "Closer to the staircase."

El hadn't seen that, but then again, she hadn't been looking.

Lanador led them back to those curtains, which were a particularly pleasing shade of green with silver threads randomly woven in. He pulled it to the side to reveal a door.

Instead of a room, the door opened to a staircase going up.

Mara went first, followed by El.

They stepped out into a grand garden. The tinkling of a fountain sounded from the corner, lifting El's heart, as did the smell of good rich dirt. It took her a moment to realize that there wasn't a roof over their heads, but more swaths of cloth, held up at the corners by tall poles.

Tall, yellowed grass covered the roof. Dirt pathways wound around the space, which appeared to take up the entire building. Many plants in pots lined the trails: flowers, bushes, cacti, and even small trees. A couple of small tables with benches sat in the corners, tucked away, the perfect place for a retreat.

El followed one of the paths to the edge of the roof, looking out at the view over the walls. She hadn't noticed that the building next to this one was only a single story. Just past it, a large open square with a lively night-market was setting up.

"'Tis a marvel," Mara told Lanador as El walked back toward the staircase.

"Aye," he said with a smile. "It's one of my favorite inns for a reason. During the summer months, it's too hot to come up here during the day, even with the shade, but it cools off nicely during the evening."

While El appreciated greenery and gardens, she wasn't a Woodland Elf, who she felt needed such things in order to be happy. She got her fill of trees and such just walking around Osirholm. This garden was a treat, though, after all the rock and scrub.

Did Mara want a garden? Did they want to try to set something up on the roof of their building?

She had no idea, though she did wonder as Mara continued to look around, speculating.

Just one more thing to ask about, one more thing for them to learn about each other.

Chapter Fifteen

While dinner was good, both El and Mara had had better.

El knew that she shouldn't suggest that Tai should hire a Gnomish cook, though she and Mara did laugh about that later in their room.

They left at dawn the next morning, following the road back out of the city.

After they'd walked a short way past the gate, Lanador had them turn back to look at the city.

The walls were no longer white. Now, they reflected the bright pinks and oranges of the dawn.

She and Mara shared a grin at the sight.

"Later on, they'll turn bright white again," Lanador told them after they started walking again. "Though if there's a long run of cloudy and rainy days, sometimes the walls turn gray."

"Where did the stone come from?" El asked.

"There's a mountain to the south of here, where the Dwarves and Elves mine stone together," Lanador said. "More than a century ago, the Dwarves and the Elves used to fight over the ownership of the mine. They finally negotiated a peace that's held." He giggled. "See, the Elves own the mine for five years, then the Dwarves do. They always spend the first year of their ownership tearing out whatever structures the previous owners have left behind and building their own."

El snorted. She knew that the Dwarves would be stubborn enough to do such a thing. She hadn't suspected that the Elves would as well.

"So there are Elves who mine?" Mara asked, surprised.

"The Umber Elves have many smaller towns, as well as a couple of cities, that are built into caves," Lanador said. "Those are further out in the desert, not just on the edges. It's the only way to survive the summer sun."

El nodded. She'd known that Nel had grown up in a smaller town that was located in caves. It hadn't occurred to her, though, that there would be Elves who would voluntarily work in a mine.

Then again, the Ice Elves generally lived in ice caves, and did their own sorts of mining.

The day passed as the days before had, with bright skies and warm sunshine giving way to clouds and torrential rains midafternoon, followed by a clear, cold night. They camped out for the first time this journey. Lanador gave them a taste of baked lizard, something he assured them they'd be having a lot of in the coming weeks.

It wasn't too bad, as the meat had taken up a lot of the smoky flavor from the fire. He had generously salted it, as well as used some green dried herbs that El thought were oregano mixed with thyme, but she had to ask to confirm.

After dinner, when they all sat around quietly sipping their tea, Lanador spoke up.

"So what's the story behind that walking stick of yours?"

El told him of the chance meeting with the Galorey, how

they'd left this behind after El had sung lullabies to them all night.

"That's a wondrous gift," he said seriously. "There are stories of the Galorey who used to live here, you know."

"Really?" El said, surprised. "Einos wouldn't survive in the desert for very long." She wasn't sure that the being could have survived even this far into the scrub, given how the moisture had already started evaporating from the air.

"This was from before, a long time ago. Before the Tiriandi Desert was formed," Lanador said seriously. "Now, these stories are considered myths," he warned. "I don't know if there's anything real in them."

El nodded. The Ice Elves had a few similar stories about the origins of their settlements, something about sliding down a magical ice bridge and a few of their people getting knocked off the bridge, landing on Annund.

"Supposedly, Tiriandi was a great kingdom at one point, full of swamps, trees that grew only in the water, and beasts that both swam as well as went onto land," Lanador said. "The Umber Elves made their home there, living on boats. Great floating cities existed on some of the bigger lakes. Then, something like your Great Mistake happened. Only it wasn't demons hitchhiking their way into our plane. Instead, the spell created a drain. The water started leaving the land."

El shivered. That sounded absolutely horrible, particularly for the Elves and other beings who depended on such wetness for survival.

"It didn't happen all at once. It took centuries for the water to all dry up. The Elves didn't figure out what had happened until the water was nearly all gone. By then, it was too late to reverse the process. There are also a few stories that when the Elves tried to fix the spell, they just made the situation worse.

So, the Umber Elves adapted. Went from living on boats to living on land. The animals either migrated or died." Lanador shook his head. "There's still a lot of magic in the desert. That's why the Umber Elves survived. Most desert creatures also have more than a flicker of magic. It was the only thing that let them live."

"And the Galorey?" Mara asked.

"There used to be large groups of them in the swamps. They weren't exactly like the ones you'll see today, as they were used to living in the water," Lanador said. "And according to the legends, they were the first group to go. They warned the Umber Elves about the drain, the evil that they felt in the waters, but the Elves didn't believe them." He shrugged. "There's a prophecy that when the Galorey return, so will the water."

"Well, Einos isn't likely to walk through this area," El said. She reached over and touched her walking stick. It always felt cool to her, even if she'd been holding the top of it for some time.

A faint tingling of magic survived in the wood, not an actual spell as far as she could see. The stick didn't appear to be unhappy about being there, in the desert, though she'd pay close attention to it as they traveled further onto the sands.

"As I said, these are ancient stories. Myths," Lanador said. "I'm not sure I believe any of them. However, even a touch more rain would be a welcome thing."

That night, El dreamed of green tree trunks covered in moss, growing out of watery trails. The land shifted frequently, as the water merrily made its way from one part of the woods to another. Umber Elves propelled flat-bottomed boats using long poles, skimming easily between the trees. Colorful birds sang as they flitted from one tree to the next, seeking bugs and the most advantageous places to build their nests. So much moisture clung to the air that it was sometimes difficult to breathe. Everywhere El heard the sound of water dripping, as though the sky had developed a leak.

When she woke, her Galorey walking stick had a slight glow to it, even when she looked at it without magic.

Was there some truth to the old tales? Or was her imagination bringing all this to life?

She didn't know. Neither Mara or Lanador had such dreams. And by the time everyone had risen, her stick had stopped glowing.

Maybe it was just her great longing for all the magical mistakes of the world to be healed.

They visited a couple of smaller Umber Elf communities on their way north. These towns were built out of brown brick, like the Gnomish community outside of Barithel. However, they looked beautifully elegant, even if the buildings were all one-story. These places all clustered around an oasis, or wells that produced clean water.

They also walked by a community that had been abandoned when the water had dried up. Crumbling brick walls still struggled to hold up flat roofs. Families of lizards, mice, scorpions, and other desert creatures found convenient shade in the remains. So while it held no people, El only found it melancholy, not sad, because there was still life there.

At the last town they stopped at before the true desert, Lanador took El to the market to load up on water skins.

Skins full of water took the shape of a glass-blown bottle—like the ones Nel had at the bar, filled with wine—and were made from some sort of leather that had slight magic cast into it. Not only would they hold water without leaking, they'd keep the liquid they held slightly cool.

"As they empty, they'll grow flatter and smaller," Lanador assured El. "They're more like water skins that way."

El was thankful that they waited until they really needed the water before they'd picked up the skins. They completely filled her pack, as well as taking up all the extra room in Mara's and Lanador's.

The next morning, they passed what she could only think of as a border. Instead of very small bushes and rocky soil, only sand covered the ground. It sparkled slightly in the sunlight. Winds had swirled it into slight ridges. The smell of dirt and sand sat heavy on her tongue.

Not the heat, but the silence overwhelmed her. Even in the desolate areas they'd left behind, there were always the buzz of insects, the occasional cawing of birds, or even the rustling of small critters hiding as they passed.

Now, she only heard her breathing, the sound of Mara's pack shifting, and perhaps the occasional breeze shifting through the sand. That was it.

It was similar to a heavy snowfall, which drowned out all sound. Except that it kept going, hour after hour.

They wore more clothes at this point—gauzy shirts to cover their arms, floppy hats to keep the sun off their heads and out of their eyes. El felt slightly ridiculous being so covered up, but she knew that it would be for the best, as the sun grew immensely hotter over the next few hours. They had to use their magic to walk over the shifting sands, otherwise their feet would have sunk in, and it would have taken hours to get anywhere.

Eventually, El found herself growing irritable. She recognized the feeling—it was close to how she felt after too many days of sunshine, without any rain.

"How are you?" she asked Mara quietly when they sat on the lee of a hill where there was a smidgen of shade, taking a break.

"Is the quiet getting to ye?" Mara asked in return.

"Aye," El said, nodding.

"Is it time to break out the bells?" Lanador said.

"Bells?" El said, looking at Mara, who just shrugged.

"Here," Lanador said, reaching into his pack and pulling out two silver balls, each hanging from a leather thong. A small slit ran across the bottom of the balls.

When Lanador shook them, a jingling sound rang out merrily.

El was both startled as well as relieved.

He handed one to each of them. "Tie this to your pack," he instructed. "If you tie it shorter, it won't ring as much. If you let it dangle, it will ring with every step you take."

"Thank you," El said, tying the bell firmly to her pack, using a shorter amount of the leather tie. Mara did the same.

When they started walking again, every now and then, a bell would ring, bringing joy to El's heart.

It wasn't a lot of noise, but just enough to balance out the oppressive silence the desert brought, so she could delight in being in such a foreign environment again.

Chapter Sixteen

It wasn't until their third day of travel that El suddenly realized that she was getting warm. Very warm. At their next break, she double-checked her cantrip, the one that generally kept her temperature constant.

As far as she could tell, the spell was still working.

Yet, as they progressed that day, she found herself grossly sweating. She felt faint, and she started to see black spots on the horizon.

What was happening to her?

Just a short time later, at the next lee, where there was shade again, Lanador called another break.

El slumped down, grateful. She tried to take a deep breath but the air burned her lungs.

"Are ye all right?" Mara asked as she sat down beside El.

El wanted to lie and say that she was fine. She suspected that would be counterproductive, though.

"No," El said in a small voice. "I'm too hot and I can't seem to cool myself down."

Lanador shoved a water skin at her. "Drink this. All of it."

El took a sip, then nearly spat it back out. "This is sea water!"

He gave her a grim smile. "No, not quite. But you need salt. We all do."

El hesitatingly took another swallow. The salt taste disappeared as she drank more. By the time she'd finished the water skin, she felt much better. Her cantrip kicked in again, and her temperature dropped so quickly she shivered with cold.

"I'm sorry," Lanador said. "I generally don't start using salt for another couple days. I should have realized that you'd need it earlier."

"I'm just grateful there's something that will help," El said. And she was.

Lanador looked at her and chewed his lip for a moment. "Hopefully, it will keep helping, all the way there. We have another week of travel, and it's only going to get hotter," he warned.

El didn't want to be a burden on her traveling companions. But she really wanted to get to the area where there might be a fire elemental. She nodded, determined to be better.

That night, Lanador found them a shallow cave to rest in. "Make yourselves comfortable," he said. "We're switching from day travel to night travel."

El knew that generally, Lanador only changed around his schedule a few days out from his destination. While she was grateful for the decision, she was also aware that it would be a lot easier on her. However, that change would make it harder on Mara, who needed her sleep.

El stayed awake that first night, talking to Mara, poking at her and teasing her to keep her awake as well.

Come dawn, she let Mara sleep and rested herself. With the

extra salt, her cantrip did a better job of keeping her cool during the heat of the afternoon.

She was concerned, though, at how fast they were going through the water skins that they had. How long before they ran out?

Lanador started them walking again after sunset. Mara was full of the stay-awake tea, and Lanador promised them a break with more tea shortly.

The desert was just as quiet at night, but El found it infinitely better to travel across. The starlight was so intense, it was lit as well as twilight. And it was so much cooler! The temperature was more like a spring day than the oven-like quality it had during the sunlight hours.

Mara grumbled a bit when they first started walking.

"Should I lengthen your bell string?" El teased after a while. "That way, you'll hear it and stay awake."

Mara considered it for a few moments. "I actually think that wouldn't be a bad idea," she said softly.

El immediately untied and retied Mara's bell, letting it dangle.

The increase in noise was instantly noticeable to her.

Huh.

Seemed that she'd grown used to some of the quiet in the desert.

She asked Lanador to tell them tales of the Umber Elves, stories of their heroes, myths of their beginnings.

Lanador appeared to understand, and was soon entertaining them with long tales.

It appeared to help, as Mara kept up the pace as they walked across the silent sands. She did take a nap at their first stop, though El felt a lot more refreshed than she had before, when walking during the day.

All through the long night, El and Lanador took turns telling stories, keeping Mara awake. Lanador pushed them to walk a little further than normal, leading them to another cave.

This one, though, had a hidden spring buried deep at the back of a slim tunnel. They each took turns filling their water skins. Lanador added salt to every skin before closing it, ensuring that they'd have enough of the precious mineral.

Mara slept heavily as the sun heated the area. El tried to sleep, but found herself waking as the temperature rose. Her cantrip took a lot more concentration in the face of such an extreme. At least they weren't trying to travel now, and she was able to rest.

They had freshly roasted lizard again that evening, a heavy meal before they started walking again. El noticed that Mara only ate a few mouthfuls.

"Don't like the flavor?" she teased.

Mara just gave her a grin in return. "Oye. Tastes fine. Worried 'bout ye, though. Yer losing weight."

El hadn't noticed that, but now that Mara had mentioned it, she realized that all her clothes hung on her. "Why is that?"

"Some of it's water weight," Lanador assured her. "Some of it's because you're using so much magic, it's eating at you. But also..." he paused and sighed before he continued, "you aren't a creature of the desert. Tiriandi doesn't like you, so she's making it harder for you to be here. She's draining you."

"The desert is alive?" El had to ask.

Lanador shrugged. "There's magic here. More magic than in the other lands," he said seriously. "I don't know how aware the desert is. But out here, close to the center, there's more of a presence. And I've spent enough time going through these lands that I can feel it. Her. Tiriandi."

El looked around, trying to see the magic that Lanador was

talking about, but she didn't see anything. She didn't feel anything either, no sort of presence.

However, Mara was nodding. "Aye," she said. "There's something here. I twern't sure iffen I was imagining it or not." She looked over at El. "I'm sorry, love. I didn't know it wouldn't like ye."

"I'm still going with you," El replied stubbornly.

Mara gave her a bright grin. "Of course ye are. Wouldn't have it any other way."

That reassured El tremendously.

The pair of them were still in this together.

And would be to the very end.

Chapter Seventeen

Now that she was aware of it, El looked more carefully at her body, as well as Mara's.

They were both losing weight. It showed in their hands, their fingers growing thin and stick-like. The skin across their necks looked taut. El didn't think their faces had changed that much, though she suspected that both of them now had hollowed out cheeks. They never undressed, so she couldn't see their arms or legs, the changes happening there.

Mara had said something about how she looked more like a person when she ate food. What had she looked like when she'd first stepped from the fire, out of the hearth? Had she been just a gaunt, skeletal being made out of flames?

It took most of the rest of the week for Mara to make the change over to sleeping during the day. El could tell when it became easier, as the glow of her golden skin rekindled and her hands regained their warmth.

As they were setting up camp just before dawn, Lanador announced, "We're in walking distance of our destination. Do we take a short nap and go out, approaching it during the day, as you suggested? Or sleep, and go first at night?"

El turned to Mara, who though for a moment, then said, "I vote for seeing it at night, first. Then going back later, during the day."

"That's what we'll do, then," Lanador easily agreed.

El found it more difficult to sleep that day. Partly it was because the heat had continued to grow. Normally, she would set her cantrip once and it would just keep going. Here, she had to continually adjust the magic, make it stronger, to keep her temperature regulated.

The other part was due to excitement. Would they find a fire elemental here? Could they finally create the ceremony they needed in order to be married?

And if they did meet another fire elemental, would that be enough for Mara? Or would they have to keep searching?

Evening brought the relief of cooler temperatures, though the night wasn't as cool as it had been. For once, they didn't have to walk with their packs. Instead, they left them in the cave where they'd camped. The only things that El carried were a few skins of water, the minerals used to color glass, as well as her walking stick.

It took them a couple of hours walk across the quiet desert to reach the area. It was located at the bottom of a basin, with slight hills all around. That surprised El, as it wasn't the most defensible place.

Then again, did the being who lived there need more defenses? They were surrounded by a desert that wasn't all that easy to cross.

Though El could see just fine in the dim light, she still had difficulty making out exactly what she was seeing, not until they'd descended one of the hills and drawn much closer.

Glass figures filled the area. El walked easily between them. She could see over the tops of most of them as well, though they came up to just above Mara's head.

Was the being who created them short? And slim, not squat?

All of the figures were abstract, not representational. At the same time, she frequently thought she saw discernible shapes, such as the woman figure that Lanador had done a sketch of, what could be seen as a diving bird, perhaps a scorpion crawling up the pitted face of a cliff, and others.

They walked in silence through the grove. The glass was mostly a whitish color, though there were some statues that had a darker brown or red hue. El could understand why the minerals used to color glass might be a welcome present for the creator.

Hopefully, the being wouldn't be offended at their gift.

There was no obvious building that they could see, no dwelling where someone might sleep the night away. They did call out a few times, asking if anyone was there, stating that they'd come in peace.

Mara insisted that they leave one of the sacks of minerals at the base of the statue that looked most like a curvy woman. "That way, they'll know we're friendly when we return."

El left the minerals used to create blue glass. When Kucher had delivered them, he'd assured her that those would be the most precious. Then they made their way back to their own camp, each deep in their thoughts.

Though they were all used to sleeping during the day and walking at night, El still found herself easily dozing, blinking with surprise when Mara woke her and it was daylight already.

They broke their fast quickly—though all of them had a

couple of cups of the tea that kept them awake—then were on their way.

El realized the moment they stepped out into the sunlight that it was going to be immensely more difficult for her than she'd realized. The heat sapped away not just her physical strength but her magical strength as well. Her cantrip faded away the moment she stopped paying attention to it.

While the distance to the glass grove hadn't changed, it took them twice as long to get there, as El had to take many more breaks.

She noticed Mara exchanging concerned looks with Lanador at one point. "I'm fine," she assured them, though she knew that wasn't really the truth.

However, she'd pushed through horrible winter conditions before when fighting ice demons, unnatural winds and storms abrading her cheeks, her lungs frozen.

She could do this.

Though she did let Mara carry her pack from then on, as it was filled with the minerals to color glass, as well as extra water skins.

Eventually, they arrived at location, standing at the top of the slope and looking down at the grove. The statues sparkled in the sunlight, the glass clearer than El had originally thought.

What looked like a flame stood in the center of the area.

Mara took El's hand. Though it was hot, it still brought her comfort. They let go of each other once they reached the statues, Mara going first.

As they drew closer, El was surprised at how the being changed shape.

At first, the figure looked just like a pillar of fire, the flames constantly flickering, as if licking the air.

Then the figure started to take on more of the appearance

of a person, with an obvious head, neck, shoulder, and arms. The legs were still fused as one solid piece, almost like an unfinished statue on a pedestal.

It wasn't until Mara stood before the being that they changed again, transforming into something that looked closer to her appearance. The flames never died down completely, though, so instead of golden skin, the person appeared to be made out of glowing fire.

However, dark brown eyes now appeared, along with the rest of the features generally expected on a face. Their legs, too, separated from a single piece. They didn't have on any clothes, though they also didn't have any breasts or other gendered parts. They stood slightly shorter than Mara, and thinner as well. They had no hair on their face or their head.

"Greetings," Mara said, bowing her head low to the being.

"How is it you're here?" the being said, after dipping their head in acknowledgment. "You are like me. But not. How?"

"I was drawn from the flames by a Mage," Mara explained.

"I was belched out by the fire under the earth, centuries ago," the being said after a moment. "No one there to help me."

For a moment, El wondered about the tone in their voice. Was that sadness? Pride? Or a combination?

"I am called Mara Fane," Mara said, introducing herself.

"I have no name," the being said. "Perhaps you can give me one."

"Harsas?" Mara said after a moment. "Harsas Fane?"

"I like that," Harsas said. As they accepted their name, their features changed slightly. While Mara had a face and a figure that marked her as female, Harsas grew more rugged, with a more solid jawline, broader shoulders, sloping down to a narrow waist. The fire dancing across their body also faded slightly, and they started to have the same golden skin as Mara. However, they didn't develop any additional sexual features.

Harsas turned to Lanador. "I saw you here, before. You came in the night, to see my beautiful sculptures."

"I did," Lanador said. He introduced himself, and El did the same.

"Did you leave the bag of color here last night?" Harsas asked.

"We did," El said, stepping forward. "According to the artisans where we live, they add that color to their glass to produce a beautiful blue color. Like the sky."

Harsas seemed delighted by the concept, particularly when El pulled out the other minerals from Mara's bag.

"Come!" they said merrily. "Let me show you my workshop!"

Harsas led them to the northern-most of the slopes surrounding the area. Though they'd searched the area the night before, they'd all missed the slim opening. Or perhaps it had been magically closed and unnoticeable.

A passage led steeply down, under the ground. It had never been smoothed out, so rocks stuck awkwardly up along the edges and all across the middle.

The heat was worse than stepping into a blacksmithing shop when the forge was going full blast. El had difficulty breathing immediately. Her lungs burned, her skin sweating out precious water. An immense weight pressed down on her, as though someone had just tied a huge invisible boulder to her back.

She trailed behind the others, making her own way down the slope, going at a snail's pace.

The area below wasn't any better. Irregular pillars of rock held up the ceiling. The path between them swerved this way and that. Lights from fires burning hotly against the walls made everything shimmer like a heat mirage.

Harsas turned to part flame again. They flitted forward, dancing between the rocks, leading them to a solid wall of stone.

With a flick of their hand, part of the stone slid to the side, revealing a large opening. Heat blasted out of the space, stealing away what little breath El had hoarded. Brightly glowing coals filled the area, almost white with heat.

It took El a few moments to understand that this was Harsas's kiln and where they made their glass. She blinked the sweat from her eyes, trying to clear away her blurry vision. Was that a workbench over there? Some crudely fashioned tools? Half-finished sculptures?

She tried to take a deep breath. Then another.

Her lungs could no longer take in the superheated air.

"Mara," she managed to croak out.

At least she saw the face of her love one last time before the darkness claimed her.

Chapter Eighteen

The quiet of the desert surrounded El when she awoke. She strained to hear anything, anything at all.

Nothing.

She knew she was still in the desert—the heat sapped at her strength. It must still be daylight out. She struggled to focus, and eventually managed to get her cantrip to work a little better, cooling her off.

Fire still haunted her.

Her skin ached, as though it had been charred. Were those blisters, puffed up on her arms?

Inside her, deep in her core, something else still burned. Would she die when those fires completely engulfed her? Flame away all her ice until nothing but bones remained?

"Mara?" El called out as she forced herself to open her eyes.

The stone ceiling of the cave she first saw was replaced with the golden-skinned face of the person she loved.

"Ye here now?" Mara asked. She reached out to take one of El's hands, then thought better of it.

El stubbornly grabbed one of Mara's oh-so-hot hands in

her own, even though the comfort of touch was quickly over-whelmed by the heat.

She held on, just for a moment, squeezing their fingers together tightly before letting go.

"Ye gave us a scare, love," Mara said. She took a wet cloth that had been draped over El's forehead, dipped it into a waiting bowl of water, then put it back on. That felt good. Until her heated skin stole away all coolness, and it felt warm again against her face, just a few moments later.

"I know," El said. "It was just so hot." She found that speaking hurt, as if she'd burned her throat.

"Aye," Mara said. "Lanador could stand it for a little while, him being an Umber Elf and all. I were comfortable enough. But Harsas's workshop can only be really appreciated by another fire elemental."

El nodded. "Why does everything hurt?" she whispered, pain shooting through her neck.

"Ye got burns on yer face, neck, and hands, just from getting so close to those fires," Mara said seriously. "Lanador has a cream that'll help cure that."

El grew very still at that.

Elves didn't get injured easily. Their innate magic closed wounds quickly.

That she'd been so badly burned in such a short time, and that her own body hadn't been able to cure it, told her just how close she'd come to dying.

"We'll be leaving tonight," Mara continued.

El closed her eyes and sighed. "I'm sorry," she croaked out. "I know you wanted to stay. To talk with another fire elemen-tal. To learn about yourself."

"I've learned some," Mara said seriously. "Not enough to

fill one of yer scholarly tomes," she added teasing, "but enough."

"Truly? Enough?" El asked.

When Mara didn't answer right away, El opened her eyes, glared at Mara, and said, "Then we're staying another day."

"No. Iffen ye stay, ye'll die. Ye got fires inside of ye now. Ye need some ice," Mara said seriously.

"How?" El asked. "Why?" She hadn't been imagining it? There were fires greedily sucking at her soul, trying to destroy her?

"Don't rightly know," Mara said gravely. "But we'll get ye out of here. Get ye to a proper healer. Ye'll live." She said it like a proclamation, as if directing El to survive.

El tried to cling to that hope.

Mara picked up the towel, wet it, and put it on her face again. "Ech. Me lass. Ye are so much more important to me than whatever Harsas could teach me." She gave a bittersweet chuckle. "Already knew that, how much I needed ye, but learned it again today."

El shook her head, though she knew better, knew that it would hurt.

Didn't matter.

"I want to marry you," El said softly. "You need to stay here, learn about yourself and your customs and your roots, enough that we can craft a life together."

"Yer a silly goose sometimes, ye know?" Mara said, shaking her head. "I know enough that I want to be with ye. That's all that matters."

"But—" El started.

"Hush," Mara said. "Let me tell ye our plans. Now that yer awake, I'm gonna fetch Lanador. He'll take care a ye the rest of the day while I talk with Harsas. Maybe get enough information for one of those Elfie books. Ye need to sleep. Rest. Tonight, we'll start walking out of here. And ye'll get better."

El wanted to object. Wanted to tough it out, as it were, to give Mara all the time she wanted.

"We'll come back," El promised.

"I've thought about that. Ye can travel with me to someplace like Barithel, where ye'll stay and explore the city while I go out into the desert for a bit," Mara said. She paused, then added, "Harsas has already shown me more of me nature. Iffen I take a different shape, part flame, part being, I can travel quickly over the sands. Practically flying."

"That's wonderful," El said. It was exactly the sort of thing that they'd hoped to learn.

"So ye rest yer mind about this trip. It's been a success." Mara paused, then leaned over and gently placed her lips against El's chapped ones, giving her the softest kiss. "We'll get married as soon as we get back."

Then Mara slipped away, before El could respond.

The fires inside of El burned too hot, too deep in her soul. They troubled her greatly.

However, her heart ached as much as her body.

She wanted Mara to want to get married. El didn't want it to be a "prize," though, for having survived the desert and nearly getting killed.

They'd have to hash it out later.

For now, healing sleep called her, and El let herself drift away.

With the twilight, the temperature started to decrease. El used the cream that Lanador provided and felt the fires slowly fade across her face and neck. Inside, though, something still burned, draining her of all her energy.

Though she had no appetite, Lanador insisted that El drink a little broth, to get some nutrients into her. He'd added a lot of salt to everything—El had watched him do it. However, her body craved the mineral so badly that she couldn't taste it.

Though full night had fallen and stars filled the sky, Mara hadn't returned to their camp. El and Lanador had started packing everything away when a bright light appeared on the horizon.

As it drew closer, it resolved into a running flame, dancing across the sands, moving as fast as a wind.

Though El was expecting it, she still gasped when the fire transformed into Mara.

Her lover had grown gaunt. Was it because she was using so much magic? Or was this more of her elemental nature? Harsas hadn't been that skeletal when they'd first met. Then again, Harsas had initially been copying the form in front of them.

"I know we said we'd be gone tonight," Mara told them breathlessly. "But Harsas thinks they can help ye."

"What do you mean?" El asked, surprised.

"There's magic here," Mara said seriously. "More magic than anywhere else I've ever been. Magic I can tap into." She peered critically at El. "And ye need help, more than ever."

"No, I'm better than I was," El protested. Her skin no longer burned. She could swallow without feeling as though broken glass filled her throat. She was low on energy, true, but hopefully getting out of the desert would return some of that to her.

"I think ye got some of me fire in ye, now," Mara said. She reached out and took El's hand.

The flame so deep inside of El suddenly flared to life. Heat overtook her in waves, coursing down her limbs. She swayed on her feet, the smell of woodsmoke heavy in the air.

"How?" El whispered.

"I tried to save ye," Mara said. "When ye fell, in the workshop. Felt the life draining out of ye, so I tried to give ye some of me own. Like I did with Thatur."

Her voice broke. "I'm so sorry, love. I was trying to help."

"I know," El said. "I know you weren't trying to hurt me." Worry filled her, and she reached out with one hand to caress Mara's face. The smooth golden skin was so warm, and yet, so comforting.

Mara nodded. "Aye. But that push I gave ye? Was a might too much. Harsas saw it. We've been working all afternoon to fix it. Fix me mistake. Make sure I never do it again."

"All right," El said slowly, though she still wasn't exactly sure what Mara was talking about. "What do we need to do?"

"Lanador, ye need to stay here for the night. Don't come close to the workshop. Harsas can't guarantee yer safety," Mara said seriously.

"But..." Lanador said, then sighed. "I want to witness fire elementals doing magic! No one else has seen something like this! Possibly ever!"

"Do you have a farvision spell you could use?" El suggested.

"I'm no Mage," Lanador said, disappointed.

"Can I set one up for him?" El asked Mara. "That way, he'll be here, far away, yet still able to witness what we're doing."

Mara nodded slowly. "Aye. That might work."

El knew that they had to do something to keep Lanador away. While he was a good person, he was also so incredibly young. He might have disobeyed Mara's request and snuck back to Harsas's workshop anyway.

El had to adjust the spell based on the ingredients at hand, but eventually, she was able to draw a protective circle around Lanador, as well as sacrifice a little of his salt and seasonings to make the spell work. The implement she'd be carrying, his "eye" as it were, was the little bell he'd given her earlier. She hung it around her neck on a longer leather thong, and they tested to make sure that as long as he stayed in the circle, he could see out of the bell.

The fire inside of her had died down a little in the cool of the night. However, El knew that it was still there, waiting to engulf her.

She reached out and took Mara's hand when everything was set.

The worried look that Mara gave her would never do.

"I love you and I trust you," El told her seriously. "I know that we'll be able to make this right."

Mara gave her a curt nod. "Aye. We will." She darted in for a quick kiss, then said, "Ready?"

El nodded. "I am."

Surprisingly, Mara gently gathered El in her arms, laying her head against El's chest.

Then flames filled El's world, and she saw nothing but the fire.

Chapter Nineteen

When the flames died down and the loud sound of whirling winds stopped, El realized that they were now standing close to Harsas's workshop.

Mara looked over El critically. "Ye'll be fine," she said.

El wasn't sure if Mara was trying to convince El or herself about that.

"Are you okay?" El said. She reached across the gap between them and took Mara's hand in hers.

"I am," Mara said, squeezing El's hand. Then she intertwined their fingers and tugged at her. "Let's go see Harsas."

"We aren't going into the workshop, are we?" El asked, her heartrate suddenly spiking.

"No, me love. Not that. Not yet," Mara assured her.

El wasn't sure what that meant. Would she be able to go into Harsas's workshop after this ceremony?

She hoped so, if only for Mara's sake.

Harsas stood at the far end of the grove of glass figures. They had manifested some clothing: an open vest and short trousers, though their feet were bare. The vest looked more like something a Human might wear, plain black, with none of the embroidery of the Dwarves. Their pants were black as well. It gave them a solemn look, like a priest. Particularly given the slight glow to their golden skin, which reminded El of a warmly banked fire.

"I'm so sorry, Elbriarien," Harsas said bowing their head as soon as they saw El. "I didn't realize you'd melt."

"I didn't know either," El said. "Nothing to be sorry about."

"Still, we have to fix this, before it gets worse," Harsas said. "Mara made a mistake when she saw you fall. She tried to push some of her life into you. Because the pair of you are so closely connected, she succeeded."

El nodded. She didn't think that was the way that it normally worked. As an Elf, she couldn't just push her life force into someone else.

Then again, Mara was a fire elemental. Maybe this was one of her natural magical capabilities.

"Now, Mara, I cannot say if you did something like that to your creator. I suspect not, though, as he never complained about fires inside of him. Correct?" Harsas said.

Mara nodded, though El could tell she still was unsure. She had mentioned, long ago, when she'd told El her story, about trying to push the life back into Thatur.

"The good news is, I think we can fix this," Harsas said. "I think we can pull your fires out of Elbriarien, without killing her."

"How certain are you that this will be a success?" El asked.

Harsas shrugged. "I've put too much fire into glass more than once. Tried to contain it, but gave too much of myself. I've had to learn how to control it, where and when to place my flames."

El nodded. In theory, that all sounded good. And as an Elf, she was much less fragile than glass.

However, Harsas had never performed this with people. He'd rarely even seen people, before now.

"And if this doesn't work?" El had to ask.

Harsas shared a look with Mara before he spoke. "You might not recover. The fires might burn out your life, far sooner than it should naturally end."

El shivered. She'd planned on having a nice, long life with Mara. Not one cut short by a mistake.

Something was bothering her about the entire setup. That they should be doing something other than trying to draw Mara's fires out of her. Her muddled thoughts couldn't determine what, though.

El allowed Harsas to place them where he wanted, standing just an arm's length apart, facing one another. Though the night had cooled even more, El felt feverish. She stared with love into Mara's eyes, and saw the same feeling reflected there. Stars filled the sky above them, making it as bright as twilight.

Harsas didn't draw a magical circle, or get out any spell ingredients. Instead, he called upon his magic. El felt it rising around him, like flames spouting on a log. The smell of burning rock filled the air, though the temperature on her heated skin remained cool.

Something tugged gently at her. When she looked down from Mara's eyes, she saw a flicker of bright red flame floating in front of her belly. It wasn't touching her. It moved in a wave-like motion, up and down, stroking the air close to her stomach.

The fire inside of El shifted. Instead of filling the core of her torso, it oozed forward, heading toward the flame.

"Good," Harsas said. "Like calls to like. The flame will call to the flame."

As the fires inside of El started to shift, her ice squeezed in to fill her core and to heal the scorched area. She instantly felt better.

However, something was missing. The ice no longer was enough. She felt cold when she shouldn't be. Still hollow, despite her own magic filling her core.

As the flames continued to move forward slowly, El found herself shaking her head.

"No," she heard herself say, though she hadn't meant to speak out loud.

"What is it, love?" Mara asked across the huge gulf that appeared to separate them now.

"No," El said again. "The fires need to stay."

"They'll kill you," Mara said. "And I won't have that."

El knew, *knew*, that Mara was correct. The fires as they'd been were too strong for her. They had to leave.

However, she reached out with her magic and grasped tendrils of the flames. Little threads came away from the main clump of fire, and some of them wormed their way back to her core.

"What are you doing?" Harsas said, sounding distressed. "The magic was working."

"The magic is working," El said as she watched the fire stream out of her body. It hurt as it passed, her skin feeling the pain of burning again. She gasped, and felt drained as it proceeded to stream out.

It leaped across the space between Mara and El, diving into Mara's core.

Not all of the flame left El, though. Some remained.

"It all needs to come out," Harsas said gently.

"No," El said. She drew on her own magical ice. It cooled off the spots on her skin that had grown uncomfortably hot. She felt it cover the flames that remained inside of her, not to put them out, but to protect them. Give them their own space to burn in, while not hurting her. It reminded her of the little cup she'd tried to create with Mara, when they'd tried to do magic together.

Mara gasped, drawing El's attention away from herself.

Blue ice traveled along beside the flames, leaving her body and entering Mara's.

"No!" El shouted. She didn't want to make the situation worse by freezing Mara. She was a fire elemental. She couldn't keep ice deep inside of her.

"Let it be," Harsas said solemnly. "Your magic knows what it's doing," he said to El. Then he instructed Mara, "Let the ice come. Bank it like you would a hearth fire."

Mara's eyes grew wide and she nodded. "Yes," she said slowly. "Can you feel it?"

El wasn't sure what she was supposed to feel, but she did reach out with her magical senses, trying to see what was happening with her love.

Just as ice packed the center of El, flames burned constantly inside of Mara.

However, now, at Mara's very core, something shiny lived.

Clear ice, grown golden, reflecting the protective flames all around it.

"Yes, that's it," Harsas said.

El felt the fluttering touches of another's magic adjusting the fire in her core, helping her bank it, to keep it alive. Possibly Mara, possibly Harsas. Probably both.

Slowly, the stream of fire and ice passing between the pair

of them faded, growing thinner, until just smoke and a few drops of water remained.

El could no longer see Mara's core. She still knew what it contained.

Fire. And ice.

Just as she now held both elements in her core.

They looked at each other, dazed, elated, and exhausted.

"Ach. Me love," Mara said, stepping closer. She caressed El's check with the back of one hand. "Ye look so gaunt."

El gave her an easy smile. "So do you."

They were both whittled down, not much more than skin stretched over bone. El wanted to sleep for a week. At least. Make someone (not Mara) fetch her food so that she never had to leave the bed. Hopefully Mara would be there for that entire week as well.

Mara looked as though she felt the same.

They slowly slid into each other's arms, breathing in the warmth and joy of the other's presence, the smell of smoke, the feel of soothing ice. They shared a quick kiss before stepping back.

"You are connected now," Harsas pronounced. "Never to be separated, possibly not even by death."

El held Mara's hand and nodded. She wasn't sure what all this connection meant.

However, she knew that now, she had years and years to explore it.

With her love.

Chapter Twenty

Though they'd planned on leaving the desert immediately, they postponed their travel for a few more days since El was no longer in danger of dying.

El and Mara spent both a day and a night sleeping in each other's arms, dreaming each other's dreams.

Lanador insisted on them eating as many lizards and other things that he could find, but El knew it wouldn't be enough. They'd burned through all their reserves. They were just going to look awful until they got back to areas with more plentiful food.

El didn't feel as though Tiriandi had grown to like her. Tolerate her, perhaps. But the desert was no longer draining her, not like it once had.

At last, El could go to Harsas's workshop. When she took the first step into that immense heat, it felt to her as though a protective barrier sprang up around her.

One not made of ice, but of fire.

It delighted El to be able to watch Mara create art with Harsas. They gave clear instructions. In just a short while, Mara pulled a globe of glass out of the kiln using a long metal rod. She started shaping it as Harsas instructed her, twirling it back and forth across a workbench. She shaped the top of it, turning the globe into a bowl.

El stepped closer, feeling herself drawn to the work. Harsas insisted that they use some of the minerals that they'd brought, so Mara's piece was the color of the ocean on a clear day, blue and endlessly deep.

"Now, start indenting it on the edges, to make a design," Harsas said.

Mara looked at the bowl, then up at Harsas. "It'll break," she said. Her golden eyes glared at him. "Ye know it as well as I do."

Harsas nodded. "But then you can learn how to fuse it back together."

Mara shook her head. "No. This piece won't be fixed after its broken."

"May I?" El asked, her magic responding to Mara's frustration.

Mara shot her a glance, then smiled. "Sure," she said.

El felt their magic rise up together, beautifully intertwining.

With one hand, Mara kept turning the bowl, rolling the iron across the workbench. She reached out and took El's hand with her other. Each of them pointed their index finger toward the glass.

A silvery spray of magic flew out. It wasn't ice. Not exactly. But it wasn't fire either.

As they waved their fingers through the air, a filigreed pattern appeared on the glass, as if etched in silver.

El's breath caught as she saw the magic unfolding. Her heart filled with love and appreciation. Tears of joy streamed down her face, immediately evaporating in the heat of the workshop. The air filled with the smell of comforting woodsmoke.

The finished piece was exquisite. Not only had the design been etched on the glass, in places it had actually punctured the bowl, making the top edge of it look like fine lace.

Mara let go of El's hand, easily cut the glass from the rod, then with both hands, presented it to Harsas.

"I couldn't have done it better myself," they said proudly. "You two are a wonder."

"Please, let me gift this to you, for all your help," Mara said, bowing her head.

El nodded. It was an appropriate gift for the one who'd helped them weave their magic together, for Harsas to have the first piece of their combined magic made manifest.

"I will cherish it always," Harsas said proudly.

El couldn't help but grin.

They were finally, *finally*, able to do magic together.

What wonders could they create?

It was time to leave the desert. For once, Harsas came to see them, at their camp, and they shared a meal together. While Harsas did need to sleep at night, like Mara, they rarely ate food as they had the fires of the earth to sustain them.

Still, they politely joined in, taking a few bites of what was served. The group shared stories of their homes and their art.

Harsas presented Mara and El with a set of beautiful glass mugs—all done in greens and blues—that they could have tea in. They also gave Lanador a tiny abstract sculpture. El couldn't decide if it was a scorpion, a woman, or both. Maybe neither. Lanador couldn't seem to take his eyes off it, holding it like it was the most precious thing in the world.

"Now, I don't want there to suddenly be a line of Umber Elves making their way to my doorstep," Harsas warned as they were saying goodbye.

Lanador may have looked slightly embarrassed at that.

"However, you three are all welcome at any time," they added.

"Thank you," El said, Mara also adding her thanks. "What you've given us is miraculous."

Harsas gave them a proud smile. "You would have found a way yourselves," they said solemnly. "And who knows? Maybe one day I'll come to your city to check up on you, and try your treats."

With a final bow, Harsas turned into a being that was mostly flame and flitted away, into the night.

The three of them shared a smile, then finished packing up camp.

They had a long walk ahead of them.

Back to the rest of their lives.

Chapter Twenty-One

El and Mara discussed their wedding plans on the long walk back to Osirholm. They quickly decided on a summer equinox wedding day to celebrate their lives together. Though it would be the busy time at the shop, they would still close for a week.

The three of them traveled as fast as they could, magic quickening their steps. However, both El and Mara were still drained from the ceremony they'd performed in the desert, and couldn't come up to full speed. They had to remind Lanador of that more than once, as the Umber Elf had grown impatient with their progress and wanted their journey to end.

When they reached civilization, as it were, the keepers at the inns where they stopped insisted that Mara and El have extra portions of the food they were served. It only took a few days for them to stop looking as skeletal, though they were aware that they were probably weeks away from full recovery.

They'd both been so changed by their experience in the desert. El learned that she could warm water with her hands. She couldn't get a pot to boil—not yet—but she was well on her way to being able to make her own tea.

Mara, on the other hand, couldn't seem to get the hang of cooling off a drink. Then again, she didn't like cold drinks. She could, however, now take some of El's ice and mold it into fantastic sculptures, the heat of her hands and her magic making the piece solid and long lasting. Before, Mara would just melt the ice and be left with a puddle.

They talked about finding a glassmaker who she could work with, back in Osirholm. El was certain that even if Kucher didn't know one directly, he would be able to find them someone quickly. Mara seemed to be looking forward to that, to having something outside of the shop as a hobby, particularly in the cold rainy months. El already had things to do, like reading in the Elven enclave and doing spell research.

The three of them spent their last night together in Barithel. Lanador didn't need to guide them along the road to Osirholm, as it was well-traveled. He wanted to return to his own small town, to tell his parents how he'd actually found a fire elemental as well as to show them his little statue. He gave El a sketch of it to show Nel.

As they were finishing their last dinner together, Lanador appeared to grow more antsy, until finally El had to ask him what was the matter.

"I know you paid me, and paid me well, for guiding you through the desert," Lanador said. He looked down at his plate, suddenly bashful. "But I'd like to ask one more boon from you."

El and Mara glanced at each other. Neither of them had a clue what the Elf could want.

"Ask, then," El said. "I make no promise that I'll say yes, though."

That earned her a quick smile from the other Elf.

"Harsas, well, they live in the flame, in the fires that are close to the crust of the earth, there at the center of the desert," Lanador said. "I have to wonder, though, how such a place came to be. There's a flow to the land, and to the sand dunes. His home, as beautiful as it is, doesn't feel natural to me, not when compared to the rest of the desert."

"All right," El said, though she had no idea where Lanador was going.

However, Mara nodded. "Aye. I feel that, too. It's a scar, where he is. Those fires, protecting a gaping wound."

El shrugged. The desert didn't really speak to her. It was better that they just politely ignored each other.

"So that got me thinking about those old myths we tell of Tiriandi, and how it used to be a swamp, until the waters got all drained away," Lanador continued.

El nodded. She remembered that oh-so-vivid dream she'd had, of the moss-covered trees, the Umber Elves poling their way through muddy waters, the constant sound of dripping.

"Is that spot, where Harsas lives, the place where the hole once was? Where the waters got drained away?" Lanador said.

"That's a big leap," El warned. It reminded her again of how young Lanador was.

"I know, I know," Lanador said. "But there's also the myth that when the Galorey return to Tiriandi, so will the water. Now, I know that no Galorey will come to the desert. It would kill them if they tried. Yet, you have a walking stick that came from a Galorey. That was probably part *of* a Galorey. A race that hasn't been here for centuries."

El nodded, puzzled. "I do."

"So the boon I'd like to ask from you is to be able to buy your walking stick," Lanador said all in a rush. "I know it isn't the same as the myth. It isn't really a Galorey. But it might be the right start. If I take the walking stick with me, everywhere I go in the desert, it might help bring the water back."

El glanced over at Mara. She knew that if the waters came fully back to the desert, they would destroy Harsas's home. Plus, there were so many creatures now that had adapted to living in the desert, like the burrowing mice, the scorpions, even the lizards.

Surely a bit more water around the edges would be a good thing, right?

Mara slowly nodded, obviously thinking along the same lines as El. "I wouldn't see the desert destroyed," she said slowly. "But a bit of rain, now and then, would be a blessing."

El smiled at Lanador. "Yes, I will gift you my walking stick, so that you may carry it with you throughout the desert."

"What do you want for it? I don't have much in the way of coin," he warned.

"You need to be in Osirholm this summer, during the equinox, when we have our wedding," El told him. "That is my price."

"Agreed," Lanador said with a grin. "And I'll bring roasted lizard meat for the feast!"

El rolled her eyes at that. While the lizard meat wasn't bad, it wasn't necessarily good, either. She'd been enjoying having real bread and fruit now that they'd returned to a city.

After they'd said goodbye for the evening, Mara led El upstairs to their room. However, instead of going directly there, she stopped at the door leading up to the roof. "I'd like to see the garden again," she said, seemingly shy.

"Of course!" El said, happy with the suggestion.

The garden was a welcome sight. Though El was an Ice Elf,

she still missed green and growing things, the vivid green that everything got in the spring. She felt as though she'd come through a long, cold winter, surrounded by nothing but ice. Now, she walked between beautiful colorful flowers, yellowed grass, and proud cacti.

Mara led them back to one of the corners. El was surprised to see a couple of pillows had been arranged there, along with a pot of hot tea and the glass cups that Harsas had given them.

At Mara's insistence, El made herself comfortable while her lover poured them both tea. The covering that would normally hang above their head, providing shade during the warm day, had been rolled up and put to the side, so the stars shown down on them. The crisp air felt good against her smiling cheeks. Smoky tea—Mara's favorite—was the perfect warm accompaniment.

They sat enjoying the peace of the evening for a bit, sipping their tea in silence. El took deep breaths, feeling the ease creep down her shoulders, lightening her burden.

While Tiriandi no longer drained her, she felt even better and more at ease now that she was no longer standing on the sands of the desert.

After a short while, Mara turned to face her. She took both of El's hands in her warm ones, squeezing them gently.

"Now, I don't know what to say, how to say this, as I've never done this before," Mara said. She looked down at their intertwined fingers and took a deep breath.

El's puzzlement started to slowly transform into excitement.

"But ye asked me before to be with ye always, to promise ourselves to one another," Mara continued on. She looked up and gave El a tentative smile. "I know I shoulda said yes, back then. But I needed more." She paused and nodded. "And I think I, *we*, have what we need now."

Mara rose up onto her knees, pulling El up with her.

"So, Elbriarien Itamar, love of me life, me partner forever, will ye marry me?" Mara said with a crooked smile.

"Are you sure?" El said, partly teasing, partly serious.

"I am," Mara said. "More sure than anything else."

"Then yes, I will marry you," El said.

Though they'd already talked about the wedding, as if it were a given, something in El's soul felt freed, a burden removed, now that the proposal had been given.

"I made these for us," Mara said, shyly pulling out two bracelets from her pocket. "A promise bracelet, for each of us."

El's heart overflowed with love. Umber Elves didn't really have this tradition, though the Woodland and Alpine Elves did. She was touched that Mara had decided that this custom was one that they could share.

She looked at the bracelet that Mara handed to her. It was made out of six ribbons that had been simply braided together.

"The red and the orange, that's for me and me flames," Mara pointed out. "The blue and the green, they're for yer ice and yer Elfyness," she teased. "The black is for the mystery in the world, the endless pool of magic we pull from. While the white is for the starlight and the moon that ye love so much, as well as the light that shows us the way."

"It's perfect," El said, tears springing from her eyes. It was the best representation of them and their lives together that she could have imagined.

She held out her left wrist, letting Mara tie the loose ends of the bracelet around it. The leftover ribbons dangled a bit, and were going to get in the way, but El wasn't going to say anything about that.

Then Mara held out her right wrist, and El made a similar knot, tying the promise bracelet to her love.

"Here," Mara said. She drew El's wrist to her, then held up her own, so that the bracelets touched. With a flick of her magic, she seared off the ribbon ends and fused the knot for each bracelet into a single piece. "That way they won't get in the way when we're working."

"You thought of everything," El said, feeling giddy.

"No, iffen I'd been thinking, I wouldn't have nearly gotten ye killed," Mara said. She reached out and caressed El's face. "Will ye forgive me?"

"I already have," El said. "If it wasn't for your mistake, we wouldn't be here. Now. Not like this."

She took Mara's hand in hers, intertwining the fingers, then held their hands up. Her ice magic rose up, encasing her hand in blue. Mara gave her a grin and joined in, her golden skin crackling with fire.

However, the flames and the cold didn't fight one another, trying to gain primacy over each other. They didn't ignore each other either. El's magic tried to give more air to Mara's flames, to support them, while Mara's flames gave El's ice something to cling to.

It didn't always make sense. But their magic worked together now.

Mara leaned forward for a long kiss. El's ice didn't melt (even though her very bones felt as though they were softening). Instead, it grew more colorful, brightly sparkling, reflecting the fires supporting it.

"I love you," El said as they pulled back, both of them a bit breathless.

"I love ye too," Mara said sincerely. "Now, how about we get ourselves back to that bed and do some more promising to one another?"

El grinned and quickly helped pack up the tea things before following Mara to their room.

The rest of the night was spent in passion and love, fulfilling their promises to each other with words and deeds.

Chapter Twenty-Two

The months leading up to their wedding were so very, *very* busy.

They'd found both an Elven priest of the moon, as well as a Dwarven priestess of the forge to marry them. Arranging those schedules had been one of many headaches they'd had to solve. As well as coming up with the vows that they'd say, as very few of the traditional promises worked for the pair of them.

Then, they'd had to negotiate a bargain between Vorwin and Frysa, both of whom had insisted on catering the event. The compromise they'd come up with had Vorwin cooking the main dishes for the feast while Frysa provided the desserts. Both Vorwin and Frysa were constantly coming into the shop with some delicacy for El and Mara to try, determined to outdo each other.

Duri made the long journey from Zaharbun to witness the event, even though both Mara and El warned her that it wasn't going to be a Dwarven affair, and there wouldn't be several days of drinking following the ceremony.

"Eh, maybe not for the pair of ye," Duri had proclaimed

once she'd arrived. "But I plan on making me way through the city, celebrating for days."

Snalgrud also came, determined to support Duri in her set path, along with a few of Thatur's other relatives.

None of El's relatives decided to attend. It would have been a journey of more than a month, and so El, while disappointed, wasn't surprised. They did send lovely gifts along: for Mara, a beautifully woven, silver shawl that glimmered like moonlight, while El received a small silver statue of the moon goddess, the crescent on her forehead waxing and waning in time with the actual moon.

She'd also invited her old master, the Dragon Azutjenga-ban, out of courtesy. She never received a reply, but then again, she hadn't really expected one.

Though El had never spoken to the Margravines since they'd kicked her out of their house, they sent gifts as well. Gyles gave them a half-dozen bottles of the most delicious wine that El had ever tasted (and Kucher assured her had cost a lot), while Ceceline promised them one of her scribes who did quick sketches, who would document the events of the day. They also gave their permission for Wyne and Sigder to attend the wedding, with Finmore looking after them.

The Woodland Elves graciously agreed to host the wedding in the Elven enclave. A large parklike space under the trees had been granted them for not just the day but throughout the night. The Elves also arranged for a group of musicians to play both during the ceremony as well as for the after party.

Finally, the day arrived. El had spent the evening at the Elven enclave. The Elves had given her a beautiful bedroom to rest in, with openings through the heavy trees so she could look out. She spent the night communing with the moon and alternating between being so filled with excitement she wanted to dance around, as well as worrying about things not going smoothly.

Fortunately, Duri had already sat the pair of them down to talk about their wedding day.

"Eh, ye know it won't all go according to plan," she warned. "There's bound to be a hiccup or two. But," she said, when El and Mara exchanged a worried look, "that's all to the good. It'll give ye stories to tell, afterward. Something to make the ceremony more special."

So while El wanted everything to go perfect, for the ceremony and the party to fall into place without a single hitch, she was also determined to not get upset when things didn't go according to plan.

The morning of the wedding dawned clear, the day promising to be warm. Nel was waiting for her when she left her room, and joined her in the pool underneath the building, carved out amongst the roots of the trees.

It was obvious that this wasn't the most comfortable place for the Umber Elf. She was used to the desert, wide open places and heat. But she stuck with El, washing her hair as was the tradition amongst the Ice Elves. Then she skipped tradition and blasted it dry with a bit of her own magic.

"There," Nel said when she finished. "Now you can put it up without a bother."

The robes El wore that day had been provided by Nel and Kucher, as their gift to her for the wedding. They'd also supplied Mara's outfit, which El had yet to see, as that was a Human tradition that Mara had agreed to. El suspected that the outfits had cost a lot, but she couldn't do anything about that except be grateful that she had such good friends.

Sky blue silk made up her underrobe, reminding El of a bright, spring day. She wore an off-white vest over that. It trailed to the ground, reaching the hem of the underrobe. Delicate silver and gold embroidery lined the front, collar and cuffs: tiny snowflakes and leaping flames.

One of the Woodland Elves came in next to do El's hair, binding it up in a tight bun with tendrils falling around her face. The tops of the silver hair sticks that held the bun in place were encrusted with pieces of opal. Gold charms that looked like tiny flames hung from them. They'd been a present from Snalgrud, who'd gone to great lengths to explain how the opals were for her ice and the gold charms for Mara's fire. El thought they were perfect.

The first snag showed up then. A Human messenger came running up, breathless and stammering, trying to tell her that there was a problems with the flowers that had been arranged for the event.

"Take a deep breath," Nel instructed the person. When he seemed about to try to speak again, Nel told him, "Now, another one. And a third. There. Better?"

He nodded and turned back to El. "There was a mix-up at the shop this morning. The roses that were set aside for your wedding were delivered to another couple."

El found herself smiling instead of angry. She'd ordered roses in both red and white to sit on the altar behind them. (Honestly, all their decorations were done in some combination of blue, white, red, and orange.) "I hope the other couple finds them as beautiful as we did."

The messenger practically sagged in relief. "Thank you for your understanding," he said. "We do have their flowers, still. We'd be happy to deliver those instead."

"What are they? And what are the colors?" El asked.

"Gladiolus," the Human said, nodding. "Pink and purple."

El blinked. She had no idea what those looked like. She glanced over at Nel, who shrugged.

"Sure," El said after a moment. "Those sound lovely."

As Duri had said, it would give them a good story to tell later.

"Good morning," El said as Vorwin came trundling into the room.

While Vorwin wore a plain black vest, she more than made up for that with the intricate embroidery done in an amazing array of colors that covered every inch of it. Her hair matched: the wild spikes looking as though she'd dipped her head in a rainbow. Somehow, though, her orange skin didn't clash with all that color.

El had met a few other Gnomes at this point, and Vorwin was the most pudgy, with ample folds of skin across her neck, broad arms and thick fingers.

Amber eyes peered up at El, before Vorwin actually walked all the way around her.

"You're still too skinny," Vorwin proclaimed. "I'm surprised you caught yourself a mate."

"Just blind luck," El said blandly. The Gnome had frequently given her a similar greeting. Vorwin had seemed personally offended by El's skinny state when she'd returned from the desert, and had been on a mission to make sure that El didn't waste away to nothing.

"It's a good thing I'm here, then," Vorwin said. "I have a special breakfast prepared for you, for your wedding day."

"Okay," El said slowly. She hadn't organized any sort of food for herself that morning, figuring that she'd be feasting all afternoon and into the night.

Plus, she didn't think that she'd be hungry that morning, as she'd be too filled with excitement.

"Don't you worry," Vorwin said. The Gnome barely came up to her waist, but she still reached up and patted El's hand. "I've got you covered."

One of Vorwin's cousins came in, struggling to carry the hefty picnic basket she held.

Vorwin caught hold of El's hand before she went to help. Nel managed to escape though, and also grunted as she lifted the basket.

A side table had been set up, a place where El could entertain those people who came to see her. Vorwin quickly spread the food out over the top of it: chicken soup with rice, a nice fruit salad, fresh rolls that were still warm from the oven (plus all the condiments), a bottle containing tea, and several jars that El couldn't identify.

"Do you know how difficult it is to get herring down here?" Vorwin asked conversationally as she reached for the first jar.

"No?" El said. Herring had been one of her favorite foods growing up, served cold and pickled, with crackers.

She gasped when she realized that was exactly what Vorwin was offering to her. "Where did you get this?"

"I made it, of course," Vorwin said with equal parts of scorn and pride in her voice. "I wrote to your parents and asked for recipes."

The sudden lump in El's throat made it difficult to swallow. "Thank you," she said.

"Oh, I know, I didn't have to do that. But I knew that you'd want a taste of home on a day like today," Vorwin said, waving away El's thanks.

Not only was there pickled herring, but also pickled greens and some dried, spiced mushrooms.

"These are all amazing," El assured Vorwin as she tried

everything. (Nel didn't necessarily agree, but then again, she'd grown up eating roasted scorpions and lizards.)

"They've got more flavor than I expected," Vorwin admitted. "Given how *beige* you are."

El smiled, not offended at the assessment.

"Still, could jazz them up a bit the next time I make them," the Gnome continued.

"Maybe later?" El said. She was still marveling over the taste of her childhood, and didn't want the flavors to be changed in the least.

"Maybe later," Vorwin agreed. "Now, normally it's a Gnome tradition for the parents to question the two getting married, to make sure that it's going to be a prosperous marriage."

"Really?" El asked. She hadn't heard about that before, though both she and Mara had asked Vorwin about Gnome weddings, to see if there was any part of those ceremonies that they wanted to adapt for theirs.

A lot (*a lot*) of Gnome traditions involved food. And cooking with differently colored food. And seeing how many shades and hues of colors could be coherently woven together to make the wedding clothes and decorations.

"Aye," Vorwin nodded solemnly. "The parents spill all the dirt, like how their potential partner doesn't season their food enough, or maybe how, as a child, they never washed their feet before going to bed. Warning them of a temper, or a lack of spine."

"Okay," El said slowly. What was Vorwin going to tell her about Mara that she didn't already know?

"But I don't have to do that with you two," Vorwin said with a wave of her hand. "You're too stuck on each other to listen to any reason."

"Really?" El said, surprised.

Vorwin just rolled her eyes and slid off the chair they'd found for her. She walked over to El, then deliberately turned her back and said, "Oh, Mara! That's the most perfect, most beautiful, most delectable snow cone ever!"

El shook her head. She didn't really sound like that, her voice so high and breathless?

Nel sitting there snickering didn't help.

Then Vorwin took a couple of steps away, turned, and said, "Eh. Me lass. It's all for ye. Yer me light, ye know?"

El couldn't help but giggle at the heavy accent that Vorwin had used. Mara didn't really sound like that. All right, except maybe when she started talking to Thatur's relatives.

Vorwin walked over and stood with her back to El again. "And you keep me warm! Come, melt all my ice away!"

Nel laughed out loud at that.

Traitor.

"As I said, you're both too far gone to see reason," Vorwin said wisely as she crawled back up on to her chair. "Nothing I say would change your mind about her." The Gnome leaned forward and whispered, "And that's the point. You won't leave one another, no matter what anyone says."

El nodded her head and said as primly as she could, "I'm glad we passed your test."

Then all three of them burst into giggles.

It was the best wedding breakfast ever.

Chapter Twenty-Three

Even though El knew that she had nothing to worry about, that everything was going to be fine, she still found herself with the jitters as she waited for the ceremony to start.

Why had Mara agreed to go along with the Human tradition of them not seeing each other before the ceremony? The anticipation was killing her!

The Elven band in the corner played soothing music, the flutes and lyre reminding El of cool summer breezes. Delicious smells wafted out from the table on the side, where Vorwin was already starting to set out the feast.

El stood in front of the gathering. The gladiolus did *not* match the rest of the decorations. Of course, Vorwin had approved of the pop of color.

Celedior—the Elven priest of the moon—stood solemnly looking out on everyone with clear blue eyes. He was a Woodland Elf, with skin the color of cherry wood and blond hair that looked like golden leaves. (He may actually have had leaves in his hair. El tried not to stare.) He wore beautiful shimmering silver robes that made El glad of her fancy outfit or she might have felt underdressed.

Khakam—the Dwarven priestess of the forge—was in all black, and El couldn't see the embroidery on her vest unless she moved. Her hair was a fiery red. Her beard matched, and its intricate braids were filled with silver ingots, as well as a few tiny hammers.

Finally, the Elves in the band changed their tune and it started getting faster, more suitable for a march.

El's breath caught when she saw Mara walking toward her at the head of a procession of all their friends. She'd never seen her love in a dress before. The top was very similar to what Mara usually wore, done in a sleeveless tunic style. But the V of the neck was cut down low, showing much more of Mara's golden skin than she usually would in public. The skirt was pure gauze, layer upon layer of reddish clouds that slipped to the side, showing bare leg underneath now and again.

Her love looked like a goddess come to the world.

But Mara only had eyes for her.

Someone had done Mara's hair in a style similar to El's, up in a tight bun with a few auburn tendrils framing her face. And was that makeup? Mara's lips seemed unusually red and captivating.

Mara reached out immediately and El took her hand. She didn't know if that was supposed to be part of the ceremony or not. She didn't care.

Mara's warm hand in hers was how it was always meant to be.

They finally looked away from one another and faced the priest and priestess.

"We are gathered here today to celebrate Mara Fane and

Elbriarien Itamar, and their choice to be together, for now and always," Celedior started with.

"Ye be forged by love, by heartbreak and by happiness," Khakam continued. "That which binds ye just growing stronger as the days multiply."

El and Mara exchanged a quick smile. The style of their wedding was going to be unconventional. Then again, so were they.

Celedior and Khakam continued to speak, each saying a few sentences that were traditional for their usual wedding ceremony. Sometimes the words and images flowed easily together. Sometimes they clashed. The moon goddess brought a message of love and peace, while the god of the forge was fiery and not to be trifled with.

El had a moment of panic when it came time for them to speak their vows to one another. What was she supposed to say? She was going to flub this, she just knew it.

Still, she turned to face her love, who took hold of both of her hands, then gave her a broad wink.

El remembered suddenly to breathe.

As well as the words she needed to say.

"You are my light and my life. My strength and support. I delight in all of you, even though you think roasted crickets from the market are delicious."

That brought a soft twitter of laughter from the audience, and El relaxed further. "I bind my life to you, not to be a burden or to drag you along behind me, but so that we can forge a new path, that is ours alone, together."

"Ye are me heart and hearth," Mara said in reply. "The reason I take breath each day. I love ye more than I can say, despite yer thinking that we should try making pickled lake greens into a syrup."

More laughter from the audience. It was a good thing that Ice Elves did *not* blush.

"I bind me life to ye, not to consume ye or be consumed, but so we can forge a new path ahead, just me and ye, together."

El started to lift their hands up, with their fingers intertwined. Mara gave her a cheeky grin and helped.

Once their hands were raised above their heads, El called forth her ice, encasing her hands in cool blue magic.

Mara's flames joined in, the bright fire warming El's cheeks as she watched.

Higher and higher the ice and fire went, twirling and dancing around each other, the blue and red reflecting and supporting one another.

With one last push, they released their magic and shot it skyward, sending it above the tops of the nearby trees. Once the still growing ball of fire and ice was clear of the greenery, it exploded like fireworks, brightly lighting up the sky. The crowd gasped, then applauded.

El and Mara had teased one another about their trick beforehand, how someone was likely to want to hire them for their next party, fireworks for cheap.

As tiny embers and chips of ice drifted slowly back to the earth, they lowered their hands and turned back toward the priest and priestess.

"Truly you have proven that unlikely pairings can be the perfect match," Celedior said, his tone a bit dry.

Not to be outdone, Khakam added, "Forged together by opposite elements, ye still be stronger than most."

El and Mara shared a quick smile at that.

"Let us see your promises to each other," Celedior continued.

El raised her left arm, where the promise bracelet that Mara had placed there still resided. Mara raised her right arm, the matching bracelet there.

They had talked over what they wanted as an external symbol of their marriage. Neither of them liked rings. And while a necklace might have been easier for them given how much they worked with their hands, neither of them liked that idea either. While El could have been talked into getting her ears pierced like an Umber Elf, Mara flat out rejected that (something about being afraid that they'd melt).

One of the most important things that El had was her Mage Mark—two silver bands around her left wrist that indicated she could perform spells and magic safely.

Mara had no Mage Mark, then again, she didn't do spells. She was a fire elemental and *composed* of magic.

Once they'd figured out that El delighted in wearing her promise bracelet, and that Mara had as well, the choice of the symbol for their union became obvious.

So with their hands raised, the promise bracelets touching, Khakam nodded to the pair of them, "Let yer promises be not just for today, but for always."

She reached out and touched the ribbon bracelets. The spell had been prepared ahead of time. Magic flowed out from Khakam's fingers, silver coating the bracelets, forging them into something new.

When the spell was over, both El and Mara had solid metal bracelets on their wrists. The designs were slightly different. El's bracelet maintained the look of a braid, sleek and artistic, while Mara's looked more like hammered metal, sturdy looking but still beautiful.

"Let no one attempt to sunder what was joined today," Celedior and Khakam said in unison.

El practically snorted at the sentiment.

Good luck with that.

"I pronounce you married, partnered forever," Celedior announced.

"Ye may kiss, now," Khakam added, not to be outdone.

There was a kiss. Sweet, soft, warm, and full of so many more promises than what they'd just given each other.

Good thing that Ice Elves did *not* blush. Particularly at the applause (and quite a few cat calls) that came from the audience.

"Let's party!" the Dwarves cried loudly.

And the feasting began.

Chapter Twenty-Four

El felt herself pulled by tides stronger than those caused by the moon. She'd wander between the tables of revelers, chatting with this person then that, before inexorably, she'd be back at Mara's side, exchanging a whispered word of love or encouragement, maybe a kiss (or three), before going to be with her guests again.

They both had so many people to see, to greet, to be thankful for. Captain Masym from *The Piebald Cub* had been there for a while, regaling her with tales of the two Dwarves and how they'd cursed during the latest storm, the great trade that he'd scored, and how inspired the Gnomes had become since listening to Vorwin talk about her cooking.

"Ye got a berth with us, whenever ye want," the captain promised again as he said his goodbyes.

El thanked him, though she didn't know if she'd ever ride a boat again. Mara was pretty set against just a few wooden planks being between her and the endless seas. But maybe someday El would get her to change her mind.

Wyne and Sigder, along with Finmore, seemed to truly

enjoy themselves, and not just because it was a day without any lessons, or so Sigder assured her. They chatted for a while about what it meant for *Ice & Berries* to be closed for a week, how people stopping by before the wedding might have made up already for the revenue they'd be losing by keeping the shop closed.

As people left the feasting, needing to go back to their own busy lives, more trickled in, particularly as the afternoon passed and the workday finished.

Everyone praised Vorwin's food. El had tried to taste as much as she could. She was too excited to be hungry. Plus, Vorwin had already stocked the cold box in the store with all the leftovers they could possibly want. Or eat. Even with the pair of them and a few weeks.

Finally, Frysa was able to bring out the desserts. There were cakes. Pies. Cookies. Crumbly pastries that were a specialty of the Dwarves. Brightly colored confections loved by the Gnomes. Even a large bowl of the rolls that had brought El to Frysa's table in the market, though luckily, there wasn't a thief this time to steal them away. Just more hungry guests.

Though Kucher had left early to take care of the tavern for the evening, Nel remained, checking in now and again with El to make sure that she had everything she needed. Snalgrud appeared to be doing the same for Mara, though the Dwarf's "care" also appeared to involve making sure that Mara had enough stout ale to drink.

Lanador had come, as promised. He'd made another trip to Harsas's home, and had brought them a beautiful glass bowl as a gift from the fire elemental. His own gifts were a pair of framed sketches of the desert, starkly elegant and beautiful. He still carried the walking stick that El had gifted him with, gladly showing it off to the Woodland Elves who thought it was a marvel.

The Elven musicians had taken a few breaks during the long afternoon, but now that the dessert table was nearly decimated and more alcohol had appeared (thanks to both Nel and Duri) they changed their tune. Instead of the softer, gentler music, they kicked it up and started playing songs that people danced to.

El caught up with Mara at one point, twirling her around the area that people had claimed for dancing. Mara grinned at her like a giddy child, possibly slightly inebriated, given how closely she clenched El to her chest and whispered more promises into her ear of what they'd do later on that night in bed.

It made El want to leave the party early, that was for certain.

They did their magic trick again, sending ice and fire up, the fireworks looking even more impressive given the darkened sky.

Just as El felt the party was finally winding down, a familiar voice spoke up behind her.

"That was impressive," her old master, Azutjengaban, said.

El turned, surprised to see him, that he'd come to her wedding.

He looked mostly Elven that evening, with pointed ears, long brown hair, and sharp features. He maintained some of his characteristic Dragon features as well, his large amber eyes with the vertical pupil glowing in the twilight, ridges across his brow and down his oversized nose, and two dozen Dragon whiskers—each as big around as her thumb— dangling from his chin to mid-chest.

"Welcome!" El said. She hadn't let go of Mara's hand, and turned them both to greet the Dragon.

"A full fire elemental, eh?" Azutjengaban asked, looking Mara up and down like she was a particularly delicious cake for him to consume.

Both El and Mara stiffened.

"Aye," Mara said softly. "What would ye have of me?"

El could hear the threat in those words, that no matter how powerful Azutjengaban was, he had better take care.

He grinned at the pair of them. "I would have you both back in my residence, the better to study you." He laughed, as if that were a joke.

"We have lives down here," El said. "Maybe we will come visit you at some point, though."

Azutjengaban nodded thoughtfully. "I know, I know. You aren't beholden to me. And I can't just take you."

El wondered at the regret in his voice. Would he really just try to kidnap the pair of them? Here? From their wedding?

"I would make a bargain with you, though," he said, glancing from Mara to El and back again.

El felt a presence at her back. She didn't have to turn to know that Nel had just shown up, ready to defend her.

Duri also appeared, standing next to Mara. Beside her stood Khakam, the priestess still carrying a heavy mug of ale.

"We will hear yer bargain," Mara said, her voice sharp as new flames. "But that doesn't mean we agree."

Azutjengaban nodded. "I offer you the hospitality of my home, for one month. I will teach you such spells! Spells that not only Elbriarien can do, but that you, Mara, would also find useful." He smiled at such generosity.

"And what are ye asking for in return?" Mara said.

"Do your magic for me," Azutjengaban said. "Let me study it."

"Why?" El asked. "Surely you have more interesting subjects to examine."

She really didn't like the thought of putting herself under the Dragon's control, even for such a short amount of time. He was getting more out of this bargain, she was certain of it.

"No, you two are unique, as you well know, Elbriarien," Azutjengaban chided. "I would see how you wound yourselves together."

El and Mara shared a look. It still didn't seem like much of a bargain, to be honest.

"Eh, it's our wedding day," Mara said dismissively. "We aren't gonna travel anywhere soon."

"Think about it," Azutjengaban crooned. "I'm sure it would be useful to you."

Duri snorted. "Yer a big ol' bag of hot air, ye know that, right?"

El froze. One didn't dismiss a Dragon that way. No one, *no one*, knew their powers or just how strong they were. There were stories of how the continent south of Annund had been turned into a wasteland due to wars among the Dragons.

Either that, or another magical mistake that had destroyed it so completely that it no longer even had a name.

Azutjengaban drew himself up, possibly growing slightly taller than El.

"Come on, have a drink," Khakam said, thrusting her mug out to the Dragon. "Tell us yer tales of might. I'll tell ye mine."

The Dragon seemed a little confused at that. El kept her giggle to herself as the Dwarves stepped forward and grabbed his arms, intent on dragging him with them.

"You'll have a good time with them," El assured her former master as the Dwarves basically steamrolled him along.

"Think about my offer!" Azutjengaban called over his shoulder as he went with them, already taking a hearty drink from the mug thrust into his hands.

Mara drew El closer. "Are ye all right?" she asked.

El took a deep breath. "I am. I'm not sure what he really wants."

"Does it matter?" Mara asked.

El thought for a moment, then shook her head. "No, no it doesn't." Then she had a wicked thought, and giggled.

"We need to introduce Azutjengaban to Harsas," she said. "They're both centuries old, and are either going to love each other or be sworn enemies until the end of time."

Mara giggled in return. "Yes, love, we should do that."

They exchanged another sweet kiss, then stood there, side by side, looking out on the party. Guests danced in the area that had been cleared in front of the band. Frysa stood in deep conversation with Vorwin, probably still arguing over flavors. The Dwarves had all piled up around Azutjengaban, and there appeared to be some sort of drinking contest going on. (El wasn't surprised to learn that three days later, when Duri had finally given up on toasting the happy couple, Azutjengaban had accompanied her the entire time, being unable to back down from a challenge.)

It had been a marvelous day, a fantastic wedding, all leading up to their own happily ever after.

And whatever else came next.

Read More!

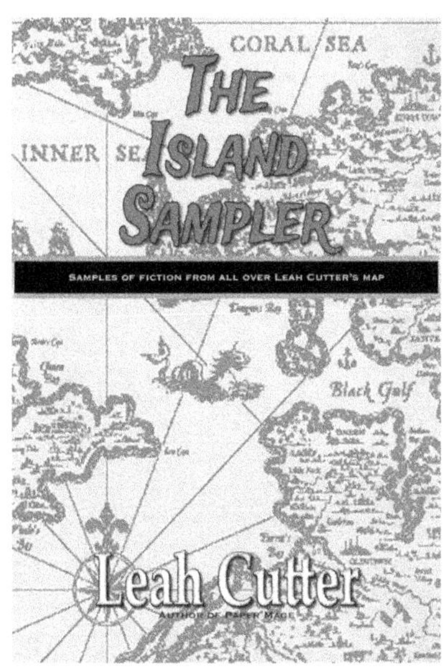

Do you enjoy exploring strange new worlds, new cultures, new people?

Journey into the various lands envisioned by Leah R Cutter.

About the Author

Leah Cutter writes page-turning fiction in exotic locations, such as a magical New Orleans, the ancient Orient, Hungary, the Oregon coast, rural Kentucky, Seattle, Minneapolis, and many others.

She writes literary, fantasy, mystery, science fiction, and horror fiction. Her short fiction has been published in magazines like *Alfred Hitchcock's Mystery Magazine* and *Talebones*, anthologies like Fiction River, and on the web. Her long fiction has been published both by New York publishers as well as small presses.

Find Leah's books on Knotted Road Press at (www.KnottedRoadPress.com)

Follow her blog at www.LeahCutter.com.

Reviews

It's true. Reviews help me sell more books. If you've enjoyed this story, please consider leaving a review of it on your favorite site.

Come someplace new...

Are you a traveler? Do you enjoy exploring strange new worlds, new cultures, new people?

Journey into the various lands envisioned by Leah Cutter.

Sign up for my newsletter and I'll start you on your travels with a free copy of my book, *The Island Sampler.*

I will never spam you or use your email for nefarious purposes. You can also unsubscribe at any time.

http://www.LeahCutter.com/newsletter/

About Knotted Road Press

Knotted Road Press publishes dynamic fiction set in exotic locations and unique non-fiction voices in genres such as autobiography, business, cookbooks, and how-to. Our authors cover a wide range of genres including science fiction, fantasy, mystery, literary, and poetry, appealing to all readers. We offer both DRM-free ebooks and print books for a global readership.

Knotted Road Press
www.KnottedRoadPress.com
www.KnottedRoadPress.com/Shop